Lola Love and The Rainbow Hearts

Sending glitter filled hugs of fabulousness to:

All the Pink Ladies who have picked up this Lola book – rock out! The best air-guitar playin' boy, EVAH – Burts. Ed-girl Lindsey for not kickin' my bee-hind *too* hard and for eating Dim Sum with me when I was sad. Jared Leto – for being *my* Tom Tootie. My Popahongo – Dad, thanks for initiating me in all things musically cool and I'm really sorry I scribbled over your Beatles autographs in crayon when I was 5! Mix tape girl for giving me the 101 on being in a band – mwoaah! Sarah Rocks – for making cool tunes, for being a total rock star and for being my go-to-girl 'bout all things guitar and girl!

First published in the UK by HarperCollins Children's Books in 2008

1 3 5 7 9 10 8 6 4 2

ISBN 13: 978-0-00-728069-8

Text © 2008 Lisa Clark

Art © HarperCollins Children's Books

Art by Holly Lloyd

Printed and bound in Great Britain

and the Rainbow Hearts

By
Lisa Clark

www.lolasland.com

HarperCollins *Children's Books*

Chapter One

Do you LOVE The Tootie?

Are you in a band?
Then we've got a seriously rockin' prize for you!

Hot punk pop band, The Tootie, have just released their fab new album, *I Thought This was Supposed to be Fun?!* and to celebrate, they've teamed up with *Missy* Magazine to offer the winner of our battle of the bands competition a one-night-only Access All Areas pass to The Tootie's sell-out tour!

For your chance to enter, send us a demo, along with a picture of you and your band rocking out, and if you're successful, not only will you get to support The Tootie live in concert, you'll be in with a chance of winning that all-important AAA pass – what you waiting for?

Go get your rock on!

33

"Lola, I must be dreaming - pinch me, pinch me!" Sadie demands holding out her petite, doll-like arm in my direction.

Sadie is far too cute to *ever* be pinched, and as a rule, I am not a pincher, but it seems my gal pal has developed what I can only describe as a touch of the crazy-excitedness, so I'm thinking that a teeny-weeny pinch might be just the thing to calm her down.

"Ow," she scowls, rubbing hard at the just-been-pinched-by-Lola spot. "I didn't *actually* mean it..."

Oh, maybe not then.

The cause of Sadie's crazy-excitedness? Tom Tootie.

Sigh.

Tom Tootie, nicknamed Tootie Cuti by...well, just Sadie and me probably, is the lead singer and guitar god for our current band of choice, The Tootie.

He is the only boy type in the whole wide world who is yummier than Jake Farrell.

Sigh. Thud.

Previously, I thought that Ooh-la-la Frenchville Charlie, the super cute-shop-assistant, was totally worthy of my crushin' and maybe even a contender to Jake's throne, but sadly, it was not to be. While I love the fact he can recite EVERY word to all my favourite Audrey Hepburn movies, according to Angel, *my* BFF and *his* next-door neighbour, he can spend an hour or more in the bathroom – every day. You couldn't *actually* date someone who took longer to get ready than you, could you?

Not really.

He does, however, make quite possibly the cutest arm-accessory though. *And* he has an Ooh-la-la Frenchville accent.

And he *will* pay you compliments, as every boy-type should.

According to Bella, my Americano gal pal and punk-trash

guitar-playing princess, when deciding on a potential boy-type to hang with, you should ALWAYS make sure that they come with a built-in compliment-giving facility, because, apparently, it does not come as standard with all makes of boy. If they don't have it, she says that you must send them back and demand a new model. Bella is significantly older than me, she's 16, that makes her an expert in just about absolutely everything.

Anyway, where was I?

Oh yes, Jake. As-delicious-as-a-family-sized-bar-of-chocolate, Jake.

He was the one-and-only heir to my heart. I say *was*, because in an attempt to rain on my pink parade, a rather pesky evil Eva Satine, who FYI, is *not* a fan of my work, is now officially dating him.

Yes, this is sad.

Boo.

In fact, sometimes I think it's even a little sadder than that because Jock boy Jake is so unbelievably wasted on Evil Eva. She is bad to the bone, badness x 100, bad, bad, bad – you get the picture, right? 'Cept, I'm the only one who can see it. Oh and my BFF Angel, she can see it too, but what with her not being here all the time – she goes to a super-swank boarding school and has to wear a straw hat that she balances on her afro – she doesn't get to see her evilness in full.

Still, I have a brand-new pink-thinkin' tude, I can play three chords on the guitar, I am officially editor-girl of my very own real-life 'zine, 'Think Pink' and I have two fabulous new be-there buds, Bella and Sadie, which, let me tell you, is waaay better than having any amount of smooch time with Jake Farrell.

I am now vowing only to spend my valuable crush time on

celeb-boys. They don't break your heart at 100 paces. They're just very pretty and really rather nice to look at – it's the celeb-boy law and everything – and they sing songs that could have been written especially for you. In fact, if, like me, you've got a very vivid imagination, those songs *are* written especially for you.

Every single dreamy word.

Sigh.

Which is why Sadie and I crush on Tom Tootie.

He is a full-time resident of Swoonsville. He's not like most guitar boys, who look like they need a really good bath. He's clean, and I bet if you were ever to meet him, he would smell of flowers and freshly mown lawns. Tom Tootie sings beautiful heart-string-pullin' lyrics and has these piercing indigo-blue eyes that aren't even contact lenses, they're his real eyes and everything. Believe me when I say, Sadie and I have a totally incurable case of Tootie Cuti fever and we don't want to ever, I repeat, ever, find a cure, thank you very much.

"Lo, Lo, this is our chance!" Sadie's voice has gone up a whole octave as she waves her copy of *Missy* magazine in the air. "We could actually meet him. We could meet Tom Tootie. We could touch him, we could talk to him, we could even sniff him!"

We could?

"Look!" She taps the magazine page from where Tom Tootie and his band mates are looking out at me from. I try to read what it says, but as Sadie is jumping up and down on my bed impatiently, I can't really read anything but I can see that it involves Tom Tootie and that makes my belly do a flip that only pretty boys can make it do.

"Miss Sades," I say, not wishing for one minute to be a fly in any kind of expensive-looking ointment, "while I am as unbelievably excited at being in the same air-breathing space as Tom Tootie as you are, and as much as I really want to know if he does smell of flowers and freshly cut lawns, we have a problem..."

Sadie frowns.
She knows it, I know it.
We look at each other and as if we're mind-reading sisters from psychic city, we both let out a collaborative sigh and say,

"Bella."

Chapter two

"No way. Not in a million zillion, trillion years. Nu-uh. No. Nada. Not a chance," Bella picks up her electric guitar and without plugging it in, plays an annoying noise that hurts my ears a little bit.

It appears we have been brutally re-buffed.

It was to be expected, but I just hadn't planned on it happening quite so early on in the whole 'Project-Win-Bella-Over-So-We-Can-Meet-Tom Tootie' proceedings.

But Project-Win-Bella-Over-So-We-Can-Meet-Tom Tootie was set to fail from the get-go.

Why?

Because in our initial excitement at seeing the ad in *Missy*, we had ran straight from my house to hers – it's next door, so there wasn't a whole lot of physical exertion involved – and just blurted out the need for the Pink Ladies to make a demo so we could meet Tom Tootie.

This was a huge faux pas. Y'see, Bella takes her music making VERY seriously. She wants to be the next Joan Jett. (JJ was this really cool guitar girl in the seventies and in the same way that I take props from retro film girls, Audrey Hepburn and Marilyn Monroe, Bella's inspir-o girl is guitar goddess, Joan Jett). Now, in times of crisis or self-doubt, the Pink Ladies each have an inspiro-girl to who they utter the immortal words:

"What would _____ (insert name of inspir-o girl here) do?"

Well it turns out that Joan Jett would *not* perform at a *Missy* gig. She would *not* want to meet what Bella terms as a 'boyband' and apparently, under no circumstances, would Joan Jett want to meet Tom Tootie either. Right now, Joan Jett is not my kinda girl.

Sadie and I pull our best glum-girl faces, complete with jutting bottom lips and everything, in the hope that it will be enough to change her mind. But we should never underestimate The Bella. She's a tough cookie. She has a super-mellow-yellow side, that's thanks to her yoga-dad who, as his title might suggest, is a bendy wendy yogini guru. But there is no denying that Bella is every inch the punk rock princess she claims to be. Today for example, her look says it all. She is working a must-have rock girl snarl painted with a thick slick of Gwen Stefani red lipstick and is wearing a Sadie-made tutu with big chunky black boots and a Care Bear t-shirt. Let's face it, a girl this cool was never going to agree to Tom Tootie Time, was she?

I almost kick myself at not taking time out to really think this through, but I didn't, 'coz that would hurt. Sadie, seeing that Bella is not planning to budge on her decision anytime soon, resigns herself to a future filled with No-Tom-Tootie-Time and sulks. As in legs crossed, arms folded, real-life sulking.

This is a first.

Sadie is usually a total ball of fun-filled energy and

fabulousness, no matter what. But it seems that everyone, including Sweet Sadie, has something that makes them glum. I have to admit that I too was feeling a li'l un-pink, but despite suffering from Tom Tootie fever too, I was actually more upset about the idea that we weren't going to rock it up.

Hold up, I'm a pink-thinkin' genius – that's it! If only I had thought of this earlier, Miss Sades would not be glum and Bella would not be playing that really annoying noise that is still coming from her guitar. Y'see, since our one-night-only appearance as The Pink Ladies, Bella has had big plans for a girl-rock revolution.

Which we would front, natch.

Now Sadie and Bella used to be in a band with Jo-Jo, a Japanese version of Emily Strange. She was a bit scary-looking because her punk-girl snarl was a permanent one. Her family run a yummy-scrummy Japanese restaurant in town and they made her give up the band to work in the shop with them in her spare time. Bella kept threatening to bust her out under the cover of darkness, but every time we went to eat there, Jo-Jo seemed so un-snarly and nearly even happy, that Bella decided against it. But Jo-Jo's departure left a guitar-shaped space in the band, and Bella says that if I keep practicing, she really thinks I could fill it. I am all about rocking out. I love it, in fact, I plan on getting so good I get to do a really screechy guitar solo – that's the stuff of my pink-tinted dreams.

"Bell, can you stop a minute, please?" I ask, trying to make it sound like a simple request and not a desperate plea from the noise police. Surprisingly, she does.

"If it's about meeting your boyband Lo, I don't want to hear it."

Oh.

"No, it's not," I lie, only a teeny weeny li'l white one. "I do want to talk about the band though, our band."

Bella puts her guitar down. Ok, she means business. I better make this good. "So, sock it to me, kiddo," She's American-o, she says crazy things like that all the time.

"I L-O-V-E being on stage, Bell," I tell her, channelling the very best persuasive Marilyn Monroe to help me deliver a prize-winning performance. "I know we've only done it once, but I loved looking out at the audience and seeing people clapping and cheering, I loved making a pretty noise with my guitar, but most of all I had loved looking across the stage and seeing my BFFs." I paused. She seemed to be listening. "I remember thinking this is where I belong. Not necessarily on stage, although being on stage is a total high-energy buzz, no, I mean, three girls of total and utter amazingness – each totally different but when put together, make the perfect team. We rock, right?"

Sadie leaps to her feet and whoops in agreement coming over to hug us both but Bella stares right at me, her big eyes fix my gaze and I know she's checking me out for fibs but that's okay, there's nothing to read because I actually really mean it.

"Right?" I ask again looking for confirmation.

Bella purses her lips and moves them from side to side as she thinks.

"I guess it would be good practice for you," she ponders.

"Exactly!" I say trying not to show too much excitement. "And it would be great exposure for the Pink Ladies if we win too."

Bella sat up. "What do you mean *if* we win?" she asks pulling her Debbie Harry platinum blonde hair into a tight pony-tail. "If we enter this competition, Lola Love, we will absolutely win!"

Bella's positive 'tude is one of the many reasons I adore her. She never entertains the idea that she might fail, yet if she did, fail that is, she'd pick herself up, dust herself off and start all over again. I love Bella. I love her even more now that she is entertaining the idea of Tom Tootie Time.

"So we are going to enter then, Bell?!" Sadie asks, totally unable to hide the desperation from her face.

Bella, like every good scene-stealer should, allows for a rather dramatic timely pause before making her final announcement. "Yes."

Sadie squeals with delight and I am beside myself with excitement as we all fall to the floor in a group hug.

"Wait, I haven't finished yet," Bella says, milking her moment for all she can get, "we enter on the basis that I get to choose the band name, ok?"

I kinda liked The Pink Ladies, I thought it had a real ring to it but this was no *Grease* movie re-run. This was the next exciting instalment of My Movie, Starring Me, Lola Love. A movie that was to be filled with guitars, Tom Tootie and pink hairdye.

"You're on!" I tell her.

Chapter three

* * * * * *

The Tom Tootie Time to do list

☐ **Form a band**
Most successful girl band of all time, me, Angel,
Bella and Sadie
Name the band – Bella's task

☐ **Record a demo**
Don't exactly know what a demo is but Bella deffo will

☐ **Get a look**
All good girl bands should have a look and Sadie
is fashion girl

☐ **Practice**
Because apparently it makes perfect. Personally,
I just like practising, because when we practice

* * * * * *

at Sadie's house, we sometimes sneak a peek
at her brother, oh and Jake Farrell.

☐ **Get picked to perform**
I wonder if they'll accept begging letters? Maybe I
could send them chocolate – everyone can be bought
with chocolate, right?

☐ **Win the battle of the bands**
Will need to work on stage presence. Bella and Sadie
have it by the truck-load and Angel positively
oozes confidence from every single pore. I, on the other
hand, need to work on it. That's okay though, because
I will find my very own guitar goddess inspir-o girl,
I'm thinking maybe Debbie Harry (super cool
Blondie front woman), who I will observe and
ultimately channel in order to 'fake it 'til I make it!'

☐ **Prepare for Tom Tootie Time**
This will involve prettification on a maaaa-hooosive scale.
I'm talking days, possibly weeks
Manicures, pedicures, new outfits and general
get-gorgeousness x 100. This is Tom Tootie after all.

☐ **Actual Tom-Tootie-Time**
As in actual time with Tom Tootie? That is just not
something I can think about right now

So far, so not so good.

I am not yet able to even tick the first thing off on my Tom Tootie Time to-do list.

This is a sad, sad state of affairs.

It should be simple. Gather gal-pals, form a band. Tick off list. Move on to item number two. At no point was item one ever meant to be difficult. In fact, like I said, it should be stupidly simple.

Well, not if you're Lola Love apparently. Because if she of the pink-tinted disposition, she being me, obviously, thought getting Bell on board was tough, well I hadn't reckoned on the curveball that is Angel.

Now Angel, by her own omission, is an attention-demanding diva. It's actual real-life factuality. She'll happily tell anyone who'll listen how fabulous she is. Not in a big-headed way, just in a 'I'm completely cool with who I am' way. And if they're not listening, she'll shout a li'l louder until they do. When she walks into a room, people look at Angel. Yes, she's got an afro the size of my house, and yes, she wears outfits straight out the pages of high-end fashion magazines, but it's not just that. It's the fact that she can demand attention without saying a world, that, *mes amies*, is star quality and that makes her pretty dang awesome, right?

Wrong.

Well it does, except for when she uses all that head-swishin' 'tude of hers to tell you that her Tambourine Queen performance was strictly a one-off and it was *not* something she planned to repeat in the foreseeable future.

"No way, Lo," she said. 'I don't do rock."

I really hadn't seen that coming. I thought Angel would be as excited as me about being in a band. We've always wanted to do the same things together, always. We always wore the same matching jumper and long knee-high socks in our first year at school together. We both ate marmalade sandwiches by eating the crusts off first. We both think spending an entire weekend watching *My Super Sweet Sixteen* in our pjs is a doable option. We have always always always liked the same things. Well, except for now that is, and if I'm honest, I didn't like how it was making my belly feel.

I persevered because, c'mon, this is Angel we're talking about, of course she wanted to be in a band really, who didn't? But so talented in the field of head-swishing is Angel, that she is even able to do it over the phone.

"But Angel," I had pleaded, when I rang her up for the fifth time to try to persuade her, "if, I mean, *when* we win, we'll get to meet Tom Tootie, it'll be ah-mazing!"

"Tom who?" she replied nonchalantly.

The funniest thing is, she wasn't even being funny.

What Angel may have in fashion know-how, she totally lacks in music 101.

"Tom Tootie, y'know from the band The Tootie? Hence the name and all..."

The line went silent for nearly an entire minute as she searched the million really important fashion designers and brand names that filled her pretty little head. "Nope, never heard of them."

Seriously, what do they teach these people at boarding school? Angel's parental is paying big bucks for her to be there. I wonder how he'd feel if he knew his only daughter was missing out on a hugely significant part of her cultural teen experience by not knowing who Tom Tootie is? It should be against the law, it really, really should.

Okay, so if the promise of meeting Tom Tootie wasn't enough to make her join the band, I had one last trick up my rather cute pink cardi sleeve. If this didn't work then nothing would.

"You can totally be centre stage!" There. I said it. I couldn't have delivered the line any better than if I was Audrey Hepburn herself in the movie *Roman Holiday*.

"I could? Even though I'd just be shaking a tambourine?" It seemed to work, as Angel's tone had changed from total indifference to one of slight perky interest.

Of course, I had not run this whole 'centre stage' business past Bella yet, but surely, she wouldn't mind, would she? She's all about the music. If all the attention is on Angel, she can concentrate on delivering a kick-ass performance. And she'll have a guitar solo. A really long one that will show any potential record makin' dude or dudess that she is indeed the best guitar playin' girl they will ever see.

I was beyond certain that I could win Bella over, and right at that moment, I wanted more than anything for my BFF to be in my band and putting her centre stage would make that happen, I just know it.

"Yes, yes, yes!" I say not thinking about Bell's response right now. "What's not to love about a tam-tam playing fashionista?" I tell her. "It would be a total unique selling point, for sure! C'mon Angel-cakes, whadya say?"

"I don't know Lo, I really don't think being in a band is...y'know, really my thing."

I sigh. What's it going to take to make it her 'thing'? "What if you were in charge of wardrobe design too?"

It's all I had left, and while I may be stepping on Sadie's super-cute tippy-toes, what with her being the customising design-o girl of the group, I just knew that she'd be okay if it meant we got a band together and got that much sought after Tom Tootie Time.

"Okay Lo-Lo, I'm in! I'm back at the weekend – get the girls together, we're going shopping!"

Hurrah.

Form a band
Me, Angel, Bella and Sadie ☑

Chapter four

The first rule of forming a band?

Don't make *any* band decisions without discussing it with your other band members first.

This 'being in a band' thing was proving to be a lot less fun than I'd originally imagined. I know lots of bands have their 'musical differences' but we hadn't even had our first band practice yet and we were already having a full-blown spat in Sadie's basement.

FYI: because Sadie's bro is in a 'serious' band (if you ask me, 'serious' equals a teeny-tiny bit boring, but the band does include Jake Farrell, previous heir to my heart, who plays bass. He makes them all the more bearable) they've got a whole studio set-up in their basement.

I know.

Nowhere, I repeat nowhere, on the Tom Tootie Time to-do list does it say 'argue with newly formed band'.

Why?

Because I wouldn't have put it on there, that's why.

But that's the thing with writing to-do lists, it only has all the stuff you actually need or want to do. I love writing lists, I write them for just about everything, but what writing a list doesn't do, which is really rather rude and wrong, is prepare you for a nuclear fallout with your be-there buds. Neither does it provide a series of practical, tip-based solutions that will get you out of the aforementioned situation.

Which would be especially helpful when the fallout is All. Your. Fault.

And that's what it is.

All. My. Fault.

"Lola Love, I cannot believe you told her she could be centre stage..." Bella is not happy. She spits out the word *her* like it's giving her a really bad taste in her mouth. "A tambourine player cannot be centre stage. That's just ridiculous. We'll be laughed off stage. If we want to be taken seriously, it has to be a singer with a guitar, not some random girl with big hair playing a freakin' tam-tam." She paces the floor and turns to me with her arms folded, waiting for my response.

I shuffle from foot to foot. I don't dig confrontation, especially when it's with my most favourite of all punk princesses. I didn't like how her accent got a li'l harsher and her face got all screwy. This was not very 'om'-like of her and I didn't like it. Stoopid, I know, but I really thought she'd be cool with it. It turns out I didn't really know Bella that well because she was most deffo anything but cool with it.

"Well?" She asks, tapping her big black boot that she carries off with the daintiness of a ballerina. "What were you thinking?"

Ok, what was I thinking? I was thinking I just wanted to hang out with all my fab friends and have a grand ol' time rocking out and maybe meet a cute popstar in the mix. Now, I was thinking that I might really rather like to run like crazy, go back home, dig out my 'weird writer girl' badge that I'd put away for safe keeping, and once again start wearing it with pride. I might now have pink hair, a pink 'tude and the ability to strum three chords on the guitar, but I was obviously not cut out to be in an actual band. I should just stick to what I'm good at, making up worlds in my journal.

In my journal being in a girl group with my fabulous friends is all pink feather boas, pink glitter sparkles and well, a lot of pink fabulousness. It would not involve kicking imaginary bits of dust while I tried desperately hard to think of how I could make everything better, really, really quickly.

Running away was still my most desired option, but my pink, kicked-in Converse had other ideas. It's like by some kind of hocus-pocus jiggery pokery, they've been sent by the pink thinkin' police to re-adjust my 'tude. Pink thinkers were not quitters. No matter how icky the sitch.

Fact. Well, that's what I thought until Sadie joined in. Yes, you heard right, even Sadie was mad at me.

"Lola," she says standing up from behind the drum kit. She has to stand up, because where she's so small and petite, she'd just be a talking drum kit otherwise. "It's not fair that you've made decisions without asking us. I had already started planning costumes – I was thinking about a Fluro –electrobeat 1970s collaboration with...well, I guess it doesn't matter now, because Angel is all fashion girl glam and will have us wearing lots of tight-fitting clothes and make up."

Now that was totes unfair, but it sounded like Bella and Sadie had already made up their mind up about Angel. I guess they just don't know her like I do, which would be really hard to do because I've known her for forever and they've only met her a couple of times. She is uber-confident and sometimes people mistake that for arrogance, which it really, really isn't. Personally, I think she uses it as a protective bubble, a way to stop anyone getting too close but that's because I know her better than anyone.

Y'see, Angel had a tough time when her parentals split up. She thought they were rock solid, we all did. They had been childhood sweethearts but then her dad got really good at all things business. He made lots of money and decided to change his title from 'husband and father' to 'player' (I know, how icky?). He now has lots of different girlfriends that he invites to one of his many houses both here and abroad.

Angel's mum was a nurse who lives in a flat right in the centre of town. Angel's mum still is a nurse who lives in a flat right in the centre of town.

Angel's world was rocked. Big time.

Oh, don't get me wrong, she liked that her dad sent her money for her to buy expensive things like bags and shoes, but secretly she missed actually having him around and doing the things that dad's should do. I say secretly, because it's only me that knows. She'd be every kind of crazy mad if people knew how she actually felt. Oh, and our journals. We both keep journals, but they'll never tell, they're good like that.

Angel would take out her anger and sadness on her mum. A lot. They'd have huge, huge rows that would always end with Angel throwing a huge, huge hissy fit – something she is *very* good at – and demanding that she go live with her dad, at once. Except, a daughter was not part of her dad's new Swank-Land lifestyle, so he offered up his love in the only way he knew how and paid the buckeroonies for Angel to attend a super-swank boarding school.

While I don't think this is what Angel had in mind, she deffo does like it there. I was worried that she'd make loads of new Poshville friends from Poshville and she'd never want to hang with me ever again but it never happened. Oh, she made new

Poshville friends, they've got names like Eugenie and Cassandra but I mean, we still talk. All the time in fact and we text each other, when I've got credit. Which is like, virtually never.

Bella and Sadie were both staring at me now, and more than anything I'd like someone to tell me how to make this right. It's at this point that I would usually call on my Aunt Lullah. She is my fairy goddess girl, my agony aunt, my mentor. But she also lives in New York – the coolest city in all of the world, dontcha know – and she has a beyond cool job designing costumes for films. What's not to love about this woman of total fabulousity?

Well, right now, I'm not entirely loving the fact that she's not here, helping me out of my sticky sitch. And I'm not digging the fact that she's not even emailable for another week either. She's on location. In the jungle. She wasn't allowed to tell me a lot about it, but I'm guessing there might be quite a lot of khaki involved.

I could channel my inner Audrey Hepburn but it really would depend on which of Audrey's characters I channelled as to what response I would get. For example Holly Golightly, the deliciously eccentric New York City girl from *Breakfast at Tiffany's* would be all "Lola daahling, walk away, you're faaar too fabulous to get involved with all this silliness." Holly is not renown for her ability to take responsibility.

While Audrey in the movie *Funny Face,* is a bookstore assistant transformed into a modelling sensation and she would say "Lola, I can't possible tell you what to do. One minute I'm being true to my art, then I fall for Fred Astaire and everything s'wonderful and s'marvellous!"

Which, quite frankly, is of no help at all.

Nope this was up to me.

"Girls, I'm sorry." I kick at yet another imaginary bit of dust, trying to avoid eye contact. "I didn't mean to make anyone angry."

"Lo, we're not angry," Sadie says coming over to put her arm round my shoulder.

"Speak for yourself" says Bella, not moving from where she's stood at the other side of the room.

"Bell!" Sadie scowls at Bella, to which she responds with a defeated shrug. I don't quite know how she does it, but with a change in tone and a narrowing of eye, Sadie can pull Bella into line in nano seconds, without ever being rude or horrible.

"We're just really upset that you didn't think these were things we should all decide together."

"You're right," I agree. I make eye contact this time, because I want them to know I'm super serious. "I just really wanted to be in a band with *all* my buds, but I took you both for granted and I'm sorry. I really am. Angel's coming back this weekend, I'll tell her I got it all wrong, she'll understand..."

Just as I was considering all the ways in which Angel *wouldn't* understand, Bella, who had received several nudges and eye slants from Sadie, interrupts my thoughts.

"Don't do that," she says linking arms with me. "If she's coming back this weekend, we could record our demo!"

"Really?" I say. "That would be awesome! We could go shopping for costumes, record our demo and take snaps of us as a girl group! It'll make a perfect story for the next issue of the zine too!"

"So, we're all happy?!" Sadie asks, looking at us both.

"Only if I'm still choosing the band name..." Bella asks before deciding to confirm or deny her happiness.

Sadie and I both nod in agreement.

"Yay!" Bella holds up both her hands for a high five. "No more decision without checking with everyone first, okay?" she asks.

I nod happily. My Pink Ladies are the bestest evah.

Fact.

Chapter five

Okay so the Tom Tootie to-do list was officially back on track. Hurrah.

And in a crazy has-the-world-done-a-double-flip? change to the viewing schedule, the one person who I thought would never, ever dig the idea of Lola Love being in a band, was actually really rather excited about it all.

You'll be just as shocked as me when I tell you.

The parental.

I know.

I can't quite believe it either.

I think it has a lot, if not all, to do with Bella's bendy yoga dad, who really is the sweetest, most chilled-out dude you will ever meet. My parental however, was not. When my pa-shaped parental left, she got sad x 100. 'Cept I didn't know at the time that's why she was sad, I thought she just didn't like me very much. And that made me sad, it was not a pretty place to be. She shouted. A lot. Even Cat, our adopted kitty, developed a 'tude just by being around her, I'm sure of it. I spent lots of days creating exciting new worlds in my journals, anything to escape the sucky real one. But then Bella, despite my initial concerns, hooked her yoga dad up with my shouty parental.

And while it shouldn't have worked, it absolutely did. Proof that the saying opposites attract is 100% factuality. I don't mean hooked up romantically, btw - ick. That's just wrong. They're adults, remember?

No, they became hang-out buds, stopping each other from residing permanently in Lonelyville. The parental still gets a re-occurring case of the grumps every now and again, which is why her face sometimes looks a lot older than she actually is, but since hanging with yoga dad, she's switched to herbal tea so she's not as jumpy as she used to be, and she doesn't shout twelve octaves louder than the rest of the human population. Well not on hourly basis at least, which for anyone within a five mile radius of *Chez Love* will tell you, is good news all round.

But while the ma-parental has definitely shown real signs of visable chillaxation, she still has a lot of work to do on her 'tude.

"What *are* you wearing, Lola Love?" she barks as I walk down the stairs to join her at the breakfast table.

See? It's not like she's blind, she can see what I'm *actually* wearing. If I were to critique my parental on this particular piece of dialogue, which, don't worry, I'm really not silly enough to actually do, I think a more appropriate question to have asked me would be something along the lines of, 'now that's an interesting outfit, what made you choose that Lola Love?' therefore giving me the opportunity to describe in detail today's creation from the treasure chest that is Aunt Lullah's old wardrobe.

I swish the skirt of the1950's style prom dress, which I've customised with a rather cute frou-frou bow and a pair of black biker-girl gloves.

"Well, it's a dress, mum," I say with a slightly risky amount of sass, "it used to be Lullah's, don't you like it?'

"You look ridiculous Lola," she informs me.

If my parental had gone to charm school, which clearly she did not, she would have scored herself a big, fat 'D'.

"So, where are you going dressed like that?" She asks, switching direction, obviously choosing to now take her own advice of 'if you can't say anything nice, don't say anything at all.' Her questioning, as always, is relentless and not dissimilar to a sergeant major in both tone and delivery. I seriously think that she missed her calling.

"Angel's back, and the girls and I are going to meet her in town." I tell her. As an ed-girl of my very own zine, *Think Pink*, I am now also able to edit my own vocab as I speak. It's a total talent. Y'see, my deletion of the line 'and we're going shopping' has now saved a whole lot of unnecessary ear ache about how I should 'save my money', yada, yada.

Yay me!

The parental has always really liked Angel. She would always comment on how 'polished' she was, not like a doorknob, but in actual appearance. The parental said that only people with money can be 'polished' and that all I had to do was look at the celebrities in pages glossy magazines to see that. It obviously has nothing to do with the fact that those celeb-types have been airbrushed to within an inch of their lives by someone with a fancy-schmancy computer programme then, *non*?

I'm not exactly sure from what, or where, my parental plucks her golden nuggets of deep, thought-out life deductions, but this, *mes pink amies*, is just one of the classics that you will hear if you hang out in the wonderful, mixed up world of *my* parental.

Thank goodness I am a pink-thinking diva of fabulousness and am able to rely on my gal-pals to make life sweeter. A girl could really go crazy around here.

"A band?" she asks as she puts another slice of bread in the toaster. She has already burnt two, the remnants of which, even Cat turned her nose up at. "What kind of band?" she asks watching me pour milk on my cereal.

"A rock/pop band," I tell her between mouthfuls. "Y'know, like The Pipettes or The Sahara Hot Nights – we're going to write songs that will make girls want to throw shapes, write songs and be pleased that they're a girl!" My parental looked at me and smiled. This was definitely a new addition since hang-time with yoga dad. Her face looked so pretty when she smiled, she should do it much more often.

"Sounds like fun," she said, saving the toasted bread just in time. Fun is a severely under used word that I was pleased to see making a new entry in the parental vocab.

"It's deffo going to be!" I tell her. She took a bite of her toast and looked at me with misty-eyes.

"Your Aunt Lullah and I used to want to be backing singers," she announced. "Y'know, like Pepsi and Shirley."

"Pepsi and what now?" I had asked, which was a total mistake because I then had to endure a whole hour-long discussion about how 'Pepsi and Shirley' were in fact, the 'bees knees.' Other such irritatingly parental vocabulary was used in the describing of how they sang with 'George Michael', whoever he is.

Now I dig musical history as much as the next all-things-retro-lovin' girl, in fact, I love, love, love all things that aren't now, but Pepsi and Shirley? Well, they did *not* sound like they needed to be added to my inspir-o girl wall anytime soon. But parental in not-freaking-out-about-Lola-being-in-a-band shocker!

Who'd have funked it, huh?

Chapter six

Today is the offical start of Sadie's new project.

We L-O-V-E a project, and this one, like all the projects before it, has yet another really snappy, roll-off-the-tongue title.

Are you ready?

It's Project Win-The-Contest-Bag-Tootie-Cuti.

Don't you just love it?

The project is deffo one of Sadie's best yet. There is nothing not to love about this project. Nothing.

Sadie and I have become PR queens in the run up to project launch day and have been surfing the web all week finding ways to make sure *Missy* magazine pick our yet-to-be-named band of fabulousity to play in their battle of the bands. Sadie said we needed an 'edge.'

"I read in a magazine how this one girl got a killer job by telling them how great she was at making tea, and guess what?" she sat staring at me with a slightly manic look in her eye, mouth wide open.

"What?" I replied. She hadn't really wanted me to reply it was just one of those kind of questions.

"She sent them a tea bag with her application. Cool, huh?"

I had to admit, that was quite cool.

"I've got it!" I tell her. "We've got to send a photograph with our demo, right?"

"Riiiggght" she says nodding her head.

"Well, wouldn't it be totally coolio-a-go-go if we did a photoshoot and then made a mini zine to promote ourselves ala my very own zine, *Think Pink*!" I'm really rather pleased with my suggestion.

I love being a zine queen and can't wait to release issue two that will look so much better if it were to include an exclusive interview with shaggy-haired, rock-god, Tom Tootie.

Sigh.

"Lo, that's perfect!" Sadie replies jumping to her feet and doing a happy dance in her sparkly glitter pumps. "We could do an interview with us and a mini manifesto as to how super savvy girls get attention without being rude."

Sadie and I clap each other's hands in a pat-a-cake motion and I join her in her happy dance, before we get to work on our yet-to-be-named band manifesto – what d'ya think?

A sweeter than sweet 5-point manifesto for our being the best girl band, EVAH!

- **Smile**: In pictures and in person, a smile makes you so much more likeable. Although Bella is allowed to pull her trade-mark punk-girl snarl during any guitar solo.

- **Being a loud mouth isn't a necessity**: Don't bad mouth other bands, even if they're not very good, just to get attention. *Show* people what you're about rather than shouting it in their faces.

- **Don't be too serious:** We want to meet Tom Tootie, and we want to be a kick-butt girl band, but more importantly, we're going to have lots of fun doing it – yeah!

- **Own the stage:** Tell yourself how fabulous you are at five times in the mirror, give yourself a hug o' love and walk out on stage and own it.

- **Remember that girls who rock, rock hardest!**: We're girls and we rock – that's the most rocking-est thing, ever!

To celebrate the launch of 'Project Win-the-Contest, Bag-Tootie-Cuti' I am finally getting to perform the best gal-pal ritual in the history of the world... shopping with your girl-gang on a Saturday afternoon.

You know the kind of shopping trip I mean, right? The kind where you get to go in every single shop, try on every kind of outfit, and end up back in the first shop you went in, buying the first outfit you saw.

Happy, happy days.

Sadie has thrown down the gauntlet, or should I say her parental-observed credit card – how unbelievably cool is that? – setting us the enviable task of flexing our shopping muscles to create four scene-stealing, award-winning outfits for our photo shoot. Seriously, I feel like I've stepped right out of an episode of *My Super Sweet Sixteen*, except, I'm 14, not 16, it's not *actually* my birthday and I'm not a precocious brat with crazy-rich parents, but, apart from that, I feel exactly the same.

There are many, many reasons as to why I love Sadie, far too many to list right off the top of my head, but one reason why I am fit-to-bursting with glitter filled love for sweet, sweet Sadie right now is that she's tasked Angel with costume design for our shoot. Sadie said that as Angel has a passion for all things fashion, it was only right that Angel was in charge of shopping. I am so glad that Sadie is my gal-pal. Angel, who has always believed shopping is actually an extreme sport, has taken the challenge extremely seriously. She has made us rendezvous at nine am precisely, under the seafront's medieval clock tower. She sent us all a text last night telling us to synchronise watches and everything.

I had pre-warned Sadie and Bella that this 'synchronised' craziness was only the beginning. After our high-five sealed 'no secrets' pledge, I thought it only right and proper to let them know that Angel was a girl possessed when it came to shopping, with glazed-over eyes and quite possibly a 360 degree head swivel. I guess they thought I was exaggerating – I'm aware that I do have the ability to over-dramz a situation – because they both sent me a text message ending in 'lol'.

A response they were both keen to take back when they found an email in their inbox with the subject line 'Shopping Rules' sent from Angel's e-account.

Well, I did try to warn them.

We all wore trainers as stipulated in the many, many rules of shopping by Miss Angel-Cakes, and we all arrived on time, well, everyone except Angel, that is.

Typical.

She arrives a whole ten minutes later and we all tap our watches in mock frustration.

"I'm sorry," she says gasping for breath. "I *was* here on time, honest, but just as I turned the corner into the high street, I saw this most ah-maz-ing sale on and there were these shoes..." she pauses for effect, "which were practically calling my name." She looks around before reaching into the bag, and just as she's about to show us these incredible 'talking' shoes, she gets derailed by her own excited story-telling. "So, anyway, I had to nearly wrestle a girl to the floor, and I would of done y'know, for these items of pure, unadulterated, pleasure inducing, beauty... Look.' Attempt two is more successful as she reaches into the drawstring plastic bag to produce the most glam-girl gorgeous, over-the-top pair of sparkly, spangly killer heels you are ever likely to see in your life.

Bella takes hold of one for closer inspection and coos out loud at its beauty. If ever there were a way to make sure these two fashion-loving girls were to bond, a cute pair of shoes, would most deffo be it. The heels of beauty were very Vivienne Westwood-esque and I could see Bella's mind ticking over as to which of her many obscure and out-there outfits she could combine her new friend's new purchase with.

Sadie, however, has a built-in practicality gene, and she's not afraid to use it. "Er, Angel," she enquires, pointing to the shoe of beauty. "While I think you're shoes are really rather lovely and all, if it rains, those spike heels will sink faster than the Titanic."

Sadie was genuinely concerned. But she needn't have been because Angel owned a lot of very impractical footwear. I've seen her closet.

"The word 'practicality' sweet Sadie, is *not* in my vocabulary," Angel informs her politely. She prizes the sparkly item of debate from Bella's clutches and we all take a collective breath of appreciation before she puts it back in the carrier bag. "These items of beauty need to be worn, no matter what the occasion or the circumstance. It would simply be rude of me to ignore their plea."

Bella and Sadie throw each other a 'Ohmystars, what have we let ourselves in for?' glance, and I smile because I know exactly what they've let themselves in for, and not wanting to pull the whole 'told you so' trip on them, they were *so* going to wish they had listened to me.

Angel reaches into her metallic pink, stupidly expensive, ridiculously over-sized handbag and rummages amongst the contents. She ignores the obligatory sticky, unwanted sweet that always manages to find it's way into every girl's bag (even a super-posh £450 version that belongs to a fashionista) and pulls out a sheet of paper.

So prepared is Angel that she has planned an itinerary of the day's events.

I am not even kidding.

She also has with it a map, outlining must-go-to shops and the quickest and most effective route to make sure we hit them all in one day. Angel's precision and organisation was in danger of making the day less of a shopping trip and more of a military manoeuvre.

As I step into line behind Sadie and march single file to our first destination, which, FYI, is Topshop, I figure it already has.

Chapter seven

"Look at the tiara!" I shout as we pass a rail of colour-splashed, sparkly adornments. It is a fact that alongside zines, all things pink, chocolate, Tom Tootie and shhh-don't-tell-Evil-Eva Jake Farrell, I am slightly obsess-o girl about tiaras. Angel already has a number of possible outfit ensembles draped over both her arms. She is attaching a set of red, glitter-girl star hair slides in the pile I'm sensing is very Bella as she casts her all-knowing-fashion-eye over the array of jewel-encrusted head-gear. She picks out the dainty one with pink sparkles for me to try on.

"Here you go, Princess Lo!"

J'adore accessories. Especially when they're sparkly and cute. They're my very favourite kind. I think it really wouldn't matter what you wear, if you've got accessories, you can turn an outfit from drab to fab in nano-seconds.

"Hmmm, it clashes with your hair," Angel says snatching it back and putting it in a completely different place than where she had found it. If I were a shop assistant, I would hate shoppers like Angel.

A lot.

The Princess Lo look has been aborted. For now at least, and I, along with Bella and Sadie, have been clicked at and summoned to the fitting rooms. While Angel and I had linked arms, I sneaked a peek behind me where Sadie was quietly soothing a mildly raging-on-the-inside Bella. It was clear Bella was not loving having a personal stylist, not one little bit.

Nobody told Bella what to wear.

"Lo, I love you and I know how important it is to you that we all get on," Bella comes up behind me and whispers in my ear, "but man, this girl has stepped right outta crazy town!"

I don't know what to do, I'm feeling all kinds of split loyalties about the whole sitch because I wanted Bella to love Angel as much as I did, and I just wanted to occupy Angel's pretty-headed thoughts with niceness so she'd be cool about being in the band. Luckily, Cyndi Lauper, of all people, rescues me from all my worry and concern.

Cyndi, I heart you.

She fills the shop sound system with her anthemic 'Girl's Just Want to Have Fun.' It was our song. It was the one and only song we had performed together as a band and it made us all break into a teeth-bearing insta-grin. I grab my girls, we link arms and we mock sing to our distinctly apt, feel good soundtrack as we parade through the store. Cyndi was right. We were girls and we did just want to have fun. Someone just needed to remind Bella, that's all.

IM to self: Do not agree to shop with Angel, ever again.

It's now 11.56am and we are in shop number eight. Cherry Tree, a cute boutique store in The Lanes. It's not too far from the store *J'adore* where Angel has a part time job. We had told Charlie, who is both the Ooh la la, Frenchville cute shop assistant and Angel's neighbour, that we would pop in and see him on our all-girl fun day but I'm not sure if Angel's strict shopping schedule will allow for anything that doesn't involve real, actual shopping, not even for Charlie.

Flicking through the racks I have found myself, without Angel's help, a too-cute Marilyn style dress that I was certain would provide my life with lots of movie-screen moments.

"Put the dress down, Lola Love. Step away from the dress," bellows Sergeant Angel from across the shop floor, where she was helping Sadie with a butterfly buckle fastening. "It's simply offensive, Lola. Put it back, it's a cotton/nylon mix for goodness sake, what are you thinking?"

I hate when she asks that. She sounds exactly like the parental. Grr. And actually, I was thinking that I would sing an old classic and sip pink lemonade through a straw in it. That's what I was thinking.

She marches over to where I'm standing, there is really nothing dainty, nor delicate about Angel, and grabs both my shoulders in a freakishly hard grip, spinning me around and sending me off towards the vintage section. I am so overwhelmed by yet more rails of fabric and colour and frills and faux fur, that I'm not sure I'm actually able to take much more of this.

"No more!" I shout throwing my hands in the air as a sign of surrender. "I simply cannot do anymore shopping without sustenance. Feed me Angel, feed me." The shop assistant shoots me a grin and Sadie, who had been trying on a far-better-than-any-chocolate-bar pair of silver sandals, tossed them aside, slipped on her trainers and bounced over to join me in the fight against hunger.

"You are both weak," Angel tells us both only part-joking.

"You choose food over shopping? Girls, I'm disappointed."

"C'mon Angel, lighten up!" Bella says putting her arm around Angel's shoulder. This is probably not the ideal way forward. In Angel's book, which I imagine is titled something like *Being a Fashionista*, fashion is not a light-hearted matter.

"Bella, I'm just concerned that you lovely ladies are not taking this at all seriously," Angel says expressing her concern, she's using her hands and her cheeks are slightly pink.

Uh-oh.

"I mean, do you really want to look like you've just stepped out of a supermarket in our photos?" she looks at us with her eyes wide open before doing that trademark head-shake 'tude thing. "Well, do you?" she asks again.

Oh no. The pressure is on, but who will give in? The battle of the 'tude has commenced. In the red corner we have Angel who is about to explode with our lack of fashion-worshipping ability and in the blue corner is Bella who is going to flip out any second now. Sadie and I are at ringside and I bite my lip so hard in anticipation of what might come next, that I make blood – ick.

It's like watching a scary movie, not that I do, because who wants to be scared-on-purpose? But you know the bit I mean, the bit when you know something is about to kick off so you hide behind a cushion. I have no cushion. I'm nowhere near any soft furnishings, in fact. So I wait for someone, anyone to speak. Except the big explosive firework display that I was anticipating, thank goodness, never actually happens.

"Girl, If it means I can go and eat a double cheeseburger with large fries and a strawberry milkshake right now, then yes, yes, yes," Bella announces. "A thousand time yes. Bring on supermarket couture!" Her older, wiser fabulousness completely extinguishes any sparks of a possible explosive in-store scene, and just to make sure Angel knows exactly how she rolls, Bella grabs a camouflage-print cap from a hat stand and strategically balances it on Angel's untamed 'fro, saluting her and doing a mini march on-the-spot.

We all break into hard and fast laughter, even Angel, eventually.

Praise be for Bella.

Chapter eight

"My feet hurt!" wails Sadie as she kicks off her trainers and rubs at her feet.

"Mine too," I agree, and collapse onto her bed with the intention of never getting back up.

"Mine three!" Bella groans at her own poor pun and joins me on the bed, pulling at the hole in her tights made by the big black boots she's been wearing.

Angel tuts and shakes her 'fro from side to side. She is a seasoned shopping pro, and today, well today was child's play for someone as professional as Angel. But in all fairness to us mere newbies in comparison, Angel has to admit we've done purrr-ritty well.

We have bags.

Bags are a sign of purched merch and ohmystars, have we purched. There are dresses, shoes, sparkles, skirts, tights, glitter, sandals, make-up, you name it; the Pink Ladies have it.

All courtesy of Sadie's parentals.

I feel really bad about letting Sadie's parentals splash the cash, surely they would go allsorts of crazy-mad when they realised how much of her budget she had spent on wardrobe, no?

"It's doubtful Lola," she says, with a teensy bit of sadness in her eyes, "I bet they don't even notice." I place a kiss her on her freckly forehead and thank her for being so adorable. It's a wonder Sadie stays so super cute and sweet and pink thinkin' in the circumstances really. If I were left home-alone in a monster house, with an unlimited budget and only staff and a big bro to look out for me, I think I might turn into a juvenile delinquent girl kicking up a storm of destruction, like Drew Barrymore before she got nice.

But Sadie's just not like that. The most rebellious her and big bro Scott get is ordering in take-outs on a near-nightly basis and doing a lot of credit-card shopping courtesy of the work-away-a-lot parentals.

Parentals are hard work, whatever shape, form and state of finance they come in. That is fact.

"So where is zee outfits of much fabulousness, *mademoiselles*?" Ooh-la-la Frenchville Charlie, our un-official band photographer, has arrived! He really is the most fabu kind of boy-type, how many boys do you know that would actually care about shopping? Charlie rules and because, like me, he knows both Bella and Angel, he is officially my partner in peacekeeping too. Luckily for us, Charlie and I are two things that Bella and Angel actually agree on, well beside cute shoes that is, so it makes perfect sense for us both to be in the same space as them, a lot of the time. Especially when there was still so much to tick off on the Meet Tom Tootie to-do list. I've only got one tick s'far. Boo.

Living up to his reputation of, you know, being a Frenchville, Charlie kisses us all twice on the cheek, Ooh-la-la. He puts down his camera which is a super-swanky digital one just like the shutterbugs use on the red carpet – he's borrowed it from his big bro, sssh, don't tell him – and sits on Sadie's bed ready to share in a love of shopping moment.

Angel talks him through what we've bought, what looks we're trying to achieve, and what angles he's allowed to shoot from.

I'm sitting in front of Sadie's full-length mirror, pulling and teasing at my pretty pink locks. I love having pink hair. Ever since Bella dyed it back in the summer, she has become my official top-up girl. There is no way I could do a dye job like this on my own, in fact, in retrospect, it would probably have been a whole lot easier if I were to just get myself a pink wig. Actually, if Bella ever had to go away, which I hope she never, ever has to do, but if she did, that is deffo what I would do, because dyeing your hair-do is hard work and a total commitment, because believe me, no matter what any fash-mag might say, it's really hard to pull off roots.

I fix my tiara is in place. (No, Angel didn't give in, I had to sneak back and get it before I left town. She may be a fashionista of the highest calibre, but I knew that with *this* hair and *this* dress – a sparkle-licious sequin dress that will put me in the spotlight no matter where I am - I needed *that* tiara. It was as simple as that, really.)

The finished look is dee-lish and the Pink Ladies, oh, and Charlie, all gasp with delight giving my 'razzle-dazzle, baby' outfit a resounding thumbs up – whoop, whoop!

"Why, thank you, ladies!" I say blowing them kisses and doing a li'l curtsey.

My pink thinkin' cheerleaders blow me kisses back and whoop with joy as I do a final twirl. They are bravado boosting queens of cool – *j'adore* all three of them mostest. Oh, and Charlie, of course.

"Come on girls," Angel claps. "We've got a shoot to do!"

"And a demo to record," Bella reminds her, beckoning me to help pull her to her feet.

"Do we get to practice first?" I ask in Sadie's direction. She nods and gives me a wink and a smile.

Not one, not two, but three whole items to potentially tick off the Tom Tootie to-do list before today is out – Hurrah!

Chapter nine

Bella Says: You're never too old to play dress up. Throw on a flirty dress with faux fur and rhinestone accessories and feel the rush that you used to get from pawing through your mum's closet – so purrr-ty!

Lola says: A sparkle-licious sequin dress will put you in the spotlight no matter where you are. Wear it with tights and heels to a party or with jeans and a big sweater on a casual coffee run to Starbucks. Razzle-dazzle, baby!

Sadie says: A cute cardi and blazer are the fundamentals of a smart ensemble. Take them from class to a Tootie concert with Victorian style rings and a punky chequered scarf. Slip into a pair of mod ankle boots and you'll be *almost* too cool for school!

Angel says: To perfect this free-for-all look, the key is to mix and not match. Pair a lacy scarf and a silky top with harder pieces, like distressed jeans and a leather jacket. Remember: anything goes in the urban jungle of style!

Angel having now slipped into her role as shoot director, was making us pull model poses that even Tyra Banks, queen of all things model-like, would be mucho proud of. Actually, now I think about it, the whole set up was like a low-budget episode of *America's Next Top Model* – Angel was shouting one borrowed-from-Tyra phrase after another like, 'smile with your eyes' and 'that's fierce' and Charlie, who was a total professional snapping shot after shot, kept saying "dahhh-lingz, you look fahhhhh-blus" after each and every one, which just made us all laugh so much that our sides were hurting.

This is how being in a band absolutely should be.

After we shot our individual photos, Charlie said, "It would be coolie to get ze action shots, si vous plait!"

As if on cue, we all shouted "Faaahhhh-blus daahhh-lingz!" back at him and fell to the floor with laughter at our own joke. It was so going to be one of those in-jokes that people who aren't here right now will never ever get.

After picking ourselves up from the floor, wiping our eyes of laughter tears and working our new on-stage ensembles to within an inch of our lives, we do what our Ooh-la-la Frenchville multi-talented boy of fahhhh-blus-ness tells us to do, well it's hardly a chore, is it? I can't believe those celeb-types who moan and groan about having to have their picture taken. It's the best fun ever. Maybe they don't have a Charlie, because I don't think they'd moan so much if they did. No one would... He's fahhh-blus.

Ok, I'll stop now.

Bella picks up a tambourine and passes it to Angel and in a moment of peace, love and laughter, they exchange a look of 'we're cool, right?' without saying a single word. I hope Charlie captured it on camera because I'm thinking that sometime in the future we may need to provide it as evidence. I loved them both in equal measure, and I love that they're both so feisty and fabulous, but it's inevitable, that sometimes, when two people who are so different, yet so alike hook up, life will get a little...interesting.

I read a letter on *Missy* magazine's agony aunt page recently – I always turn straight to the advice pages, they're the best bit – and this girl had written in saying how her friends were so different and she wasn't sure if they'd get on, what should she do? The agony aunt, who I love, said that life would be pretty boring if we were all the same and that we don't have to always be into the same stuff to get on. Which isn't a whole lot of different to my own sitch right now, it's just that in Lola's land, I'd really like life to be as sweet as sugar, all the time and for my gal-pals to get on, all of the time too. Is that really too much to ask?

That's why, right now, I am splashing around in the knowledge that these two are on a stage, all be it a teeny tiny one in Sadie's basement, together, and they're smiling at each other. And laughing.

Bella, Sades and I have been working on a tune that we really quite like so we play it through once, just so Angel can get the idea and then play it again with Angel tap-tappin' her tam-tam.

"Go girl!" Bella shouts across the stage as Angel shakes her bee-hind in time to the tambourine. If I do say so myself we've really got it going on, well, until Angel tries to sing. There really are many things Angel is good at, shopping, as we witnessed, today, putting cute outfits together and the ability to make me feel fabulous even when she's away at boarding school, but singing?

Singing is not on that list. I bite back a sneaky giggle as she tries to mimic the words, like my dad used to do when he listened to a song he didn't know on the radio. Just like my dad, Angel doesn't know the words, so she replaces them with her own. It is all I can do not to break out in a full-on laughter fest, but Bella throws me a look that says 'Lo, don't encourage her.'

"Er, Angel, look..." Bella says stopping mid-song and watching in astonishment as Angel carries on tapping and shaking and sing completely inaudible words. "I love what you've done with the outfits, we are Rocksville City, USA, but seriously, can you leave the singing to me?"

Angel was shocked, not because Bella was telling her to stop singing, but because she really, honestly didn't even know she was doing it. "Of course, Bell," Angel says, not really knowing what the problem was. After a few run throughs, I say few, it was more like ten because Bella is a total perfectionist, minus Angel's tone deaf attempt to join in, Bella presses the record button and counts us in.

"Okay girls, y'ready?" She yells. I fiddle with a knob on the guitar, I don't know what it does exactly, but I've seen guitar playin' types do it, and as I'm now a proper guitar playin' type, I do it too. Not too much though, I don't want to mess it up, and nod in Bella's direction.

"A 1, a 1, a 1, 2, 3, 4!" On Bella's cue we make a whole lot of punk pop noise while Bella sings a self-penned song about being the 'girl of the moment.'

When we play it back and I get goosebumps and tingles and the hair on the back of my neck stands on end, because it's us.

Bella, Angel, Sadie and Lola Love.

It's us, making music. We're making music and we're in a band and we're now sitting in front of a speaker, listening to our demo.

Un-blimmin'-believeable.

FYI: A demo, I have now found out, is short for demonstration as in a demonstration of what you can do, as in 'c'mon then, show us what'cha got. And we've deffo done that. In fact, if I were to borrow a Bella American-o phrase, we have 'brought it'. We're not polished and perfect, as much as Bella would really rather like us to be, but it's raw and fun-sounding. If I were a girl sitting at home listening to the radio and this song came on, it would deffo fill me to the brim with go-girl goodness.

Which, if you ask me, deserves a round of high fives and shape-throwing dances of sheer, total pink-tinted happiness.

The thing is, we still didn't have a name. I didn't want Bella to think I was taking over or anything, but I really wanted us to have a kick-ass name, something that would make us stand out from the other applicants, something with staying power, something, y'know, good.

"Bell," I say as I watch her take our 'demo' from the recorder and place it in a case, "you know you said you wanted to name the band?"

"Yeah-huh," she says, pulling the lid off a Sharpie pen with her teeth and writing on the plastic casing.

"Well, have you decided yet?" I wince a little as I wait for her response.

She turns on her heel and holds the plastic demo up close to my face in a product placement style manoeuvre.

I struggle to read her swirly-whirly writing that should really belong to a boy.

"So, whad'ya reckon?" She asks.

"The Rainbow Hearts," I read.

Then I say it out loud to hear what it sounds like. "Please welcome on stage – The Rainbow Hearts!"

Angel Sadie and I look at each other, pull various lip shapes at each other, before all three of us decided on huge, lip stretchin' mega-watt grins. Charlie, sensing a career defining, picture-perfect moment happening right before his Ooh-la-la Frenchville eyes, calls to us, tells us to say 'The Rainbow Hearts' and snaps what he claims to be our future cover art.

Fahhhhhh-blus.

Form a band   ☑
Name the band   ☑
Record a demo   ☑
Get a look   ☑
Practice   ☑

Chapter ten

The Tom Tootie to-do list is looking significantly better now that it has five decent-sized, written-in-marker ticks on it. There's something very satisfying about ticking off things you've achieved on a list, if only I'd written a list for everything I did yesterday. If I had of done, then I would have an entire page of A4, at least, filled with ticks right now.

I was quite the creative girl, putting together a rather fabulous – if I do say so myself - press pack for our *Missy* magazine 'Meet Tom Tootie' entry. Sadie was right, you do have to be totally you-nique if you want to stand out from the crowd, so putting together a mini-mag to accompany our entry is just a nice li'l touch to let the people at Missy know we really want to win. I'm tempted to still add a bar of chocolate, y'know, just in case. I checked the masthead at the front of the mag, the bit where they list staff names and what they do, and they were all girls, and there's not a girl in the world who can resist chocolate, is there?

Not that our Rainbow Hearts demo and press pack won't wow them alone, because let me tell you, it really, really will. I printed off Charlie's awesome pictures – they were so good, he really captured us and we looked totally ready to head up Bella's girl rock revolution – we were rockin'. I cut and pasted zine page layouts onto pink paper, I tried out my journo-girl skills by interviewing Sades, Bell and Angel-cakes for our mock interview and I even designed a Rainbow Heart logo, which consisted of a rainbow and a heart, funnily enough.

Sadie and I were going to post the package of love-filled fabulousness after school today, but I kept having nightmarish visions that Evil Eva got a hold of it, she had a history of taking things that didn't belong to her, before we got to the post box and that was *not* a risk I was willing to take. So, instead, the Pink Ladies and I decided to post it together in a 'go-rainbow hearts-go!' ritual of loveliness.

Before Angel's ma-parental had to drive her back to the super-swank boarding school, we all went to the post box and kissed the package good luck, with Angel leaving a big, pink lip-glossed smooch on the back. We all said our 'we're The Rainbow Hearts and we rock and rule!' affirmation and pushed it in the red, letter box.

There.

All that stood between Tom Tootie Time and The Rainbow Hearts now was the small matter of being picked, oh, and winning the battle of the bands too. Actually, they're both quite substantial sized things, aren't they? Some might even call them obstacles, not me though. I'm a pink thinkin' lady of fabulousity starring in Life is a Movie, Starring Me, Lola Love. What kind of movie would it be without obstacles to overcome? Every leading lady has them and how she deals with them is what really makes the movie a box office hit.

Although sometimes, what you think might be a huge totally un-get-overable brick wall of an obstacle, like f'rinstance, getting a slightly neurotic ma-parental with a tendency to shout a lot to agree to you going to a gig on a school night, turns out to be the most easy-breezy walk in the park on a sunshiney day.

I know.

I'm going to a gig, on a on a school night and the ma-parental has not, I repeat not, gone a hundred kinds of crazy about it. I had polished up my very best negotiation skills to win her over on this one. When Bella had told me that one of her favourite girl-groups, Baby Doll were playing at The Pier, I was excited. When she told me it was planned for a school night? Not so much. The ma-parental had lightened up, I thought, but not t*hat* much.

I had contemplated sneaking out, but the most rebellious I get is dying my hair pink. What can I say? I'm bad at being bad, which ultimately makes me good in so many ways. Good girls rule. So instead, I prepared an offer of doing the washing up for a week, tidying my room *and* cooking tea for an entire month. If that didn't win her over then nothing would. I'm a good cook, she is not.

But I hadn't needed them, not one of them, because the conversation, which I had to write in my journal for future reference, went like this:

Me: Mum, there's this really cool band, Baby Doll are playing at The Pier next week...

Ma–parental: What day?

Me: Monday

Ma–parental: What time does it finish?

Me: 9.30 I think.

Ma-parental: Is Bella going?

Me: Yep, it was her idea. She thinks it would be great research for us to go see a girl-group live...

Ma-parental: Well, just as long as you're back by 9.30, otherwise I'll call the police.

No, I can't quite believe it either, and if she hadn't added that last bit about calling the police, I would have sworn blind that this woman standing before me in an all-in-black tracksuit combo, was not my ma-parental. I'm still keeping a tight hold on my negotiation tools though, just in case.

So I'm off to see Baby Doll, with my gal-pals on a school night, which is beyond exciting, there's just the small, inconvenient matter of having to go to school first. It's incredibly frustrating for a soon-to-be guitar goddess like myself to have to partake in mundane tasks like schooling, especially when my lessons in all things guitar goddess like will be learned from the red-lip pouting Aubrey Silk, lead singer and guitarist of Baby Doll. Bella is a huge fan and has a signed poster of her on her boudoir wall. She says tonight will be an education in everything a guitar-girl group should be.

"It's a shame Angel can't stay for the gig," Bella had said as we had waved Angel off to Swanksville High, "I'm worried she's not so au fait with all things rock as we are, and Baby Doll would have been the perfect 101 to girl rock for her."

I had nodded, because Bella was right, Angel really wasn't into rock, and although she was digging the stylin' and directing and general prettification element of being a band, I'm not sure she was really feeling the music, and if the interviews that I've read in Bella's *Rawk Weekly* were anything to go by, musical differences can make or break a band. I push any thoughts of breaking up before we've even started, to the back of my mind and concentrate on the matter at hand.

Maths.

Chapter eleven

I love Maths.

In fact if I could, I would make Maths last all day.

Not because I'm any good at it, mind you. If the truth be told, I'm actually shockingly bad x 100 at it, as Miss Posey, Maths teacher and pain inflictor would be more than happy to confirm. But I love Miss Posey, despite her acute angles and big unfathomable equations because she insists that we sit in alphabetical order and luckily for me, no one has a last name beginning with g, h, i, j or even k, which means a whole forty five, dee-lish minutes spent sitting within licking distance of beautiful Jake Farrell.

You'd better make that forty minutes, he's always late.

But he's worth the wait. His entrance is befitting of an action hero – all reverberating door slams and tricky desk-jump manoeuvres. Throwing his over-sized sports bag to the floor, he slides into his chair. The overall performance was distinctively lacking in poise and grace but with looks like his, he couldn't fail to be a star. I'm trying not to crush on him anymore, what with him dating Evil Eva and all, but he doesn't make it easy.

He makes himself comfy in the chair next to mine and

whispers in my ear, his breath is warm and tickles my senses.

"Lola, can I copy your homework please?"

Okay, so it's not exactly sweet nothings, but it was contact. Since meeting him at Sadie's house – he plays in Sadie's bro's band, I know, jock-boy *and* guitar boy...sigh – he now knows that I actually exist and despite any bad-mouthing from his poor taste in current girl-types, he's always really nice to me. Well, he's asked to copy my homework, which is a huge leap forward from not knowing you actually exist, right?

I slide him my book, opening it at the correct page, because well, I'm good like that. I'm oblivious to Miss Posey and her equilateral triangles because I'm watching Jake. His arm is so close to mine that it's all I can do not to reach out and touch it. As he rubs at a mistake viciously with an eraser, I can smell him. It's a heady mix of sport-boy sweat and deodorant. On anyone else, there is a good chance that this combo would induce vomit, but on him, well, on him...it was ok, because he was Jake Farrell, and no matter how much I try to tell myself otherwise, he is still the real-life heir to my heart.

He has caught me looking, so I turn away really quickly and twirl a strand of hair around my finger. Cher in the movie *Clueless* – one of the best chick flicks, ever btw – says that this is such a good look if you can pull it off, I am not Cher, but I am a li'l clueless it seems as I have made a great big knot in my candyfloss pink hair. I fight with the offending matt of hair and look back to see Jake smiling.

He smiles a tooth and gum smile. A smile you would absolutely expect, no, demand, the captain of the football team to have and I savour this sweet pleasure, as he places my book back in front of me and whispers "Thanks Lola."

Sigh.

Thud.

Miss Posey has turned to the board to write up some crazy sum and that's my cue to catch up on essential reading - *Missy* magazine. I'm working on pink thinkin' visualisation, where I look at the picture of Tom Tootie and create a picture of The Rainbow Hearts in my head, we're rockin' out and winning the battle of the bands, if I do it often enough I'm completely convinced it'll make it come true. It's like the very best kind of daydreaming, something I believe Maths class was actually invented for.

"Are you entering?" Jake whispers pointing to the competition page. I hadn't realised Jake was reading over my shoulder.

"Yeah, we are!" I reply enthusiastically impressed by his attention to my competition entering abilities. I was about to tell him all about how we were called The Rainbow Hearts and how we had made a demo and had cute on-stage outfits – all the really important stuff, when Jake Farrell, in one single sentence was able to bring Project Win The Contest, Meet Tom Tootie to a break-screeching, grinding halt.

"Cool, so is Eva!"

My pink-thinkin' bubble had burst.

"But, she's not even in a band!" I whine.

"She is now!" He says really not sensitive to the pain I was currently feeling, "think you and the girls may have inspired her when you played at our gig!"

Brilliant.

Just brilliant.

If you haven't met Eva, you'll deffo know someone like her. She's the kind of girl who can make you feel like you're three years old and have just been told that you can't play in the sandbox, simply by looking at you. I hate dissin' on girlkind, but she's really not a very nice addition to the sisterhood. If I thought she had actually been inspired to set up a band just because she'd seen me and the Pink Ladies rockin' out, I would be really okay with that, in fact, I'd even be inclined to get my happy on, because it'd mean evil Eva wasn't so evil after all. But I'm sorry, I'm having such major-league trouble believing that could ever actually be true.

Jake, despite imparting such bubble-bursting news of badness into my land o' pink, does redeem himself, only slightly though, by offering to put Sadie, Bella and I on the guest list for the Baby Doll gig tonight. Apparently he knows someone on the door. Quite frankly, under the circumstances, it was the blimmin' least he could do.

When I meet Sadie after class, no matter how hard I try to rearrange it, my face is completely the wrong side of happy.

"What d'ya know, Lo?" Sadie asks, giving me a friendly jab on the arm and offering up a chunk of chocolate. She digs the poetry and would love nothing more than to talk in rhyme, all of the time.

"Something's up, isn't it?" says Sadie searching my face for clues, "c'mon, spill."

"Well do you want the good news, or the bad news?" I say, enjoying the insta-sugar-rush that you only get from chocolate - yum.

"Ohh, the good news, please!" Sadie was a pink-thinkin' supremo.

"Jake Farrell has said he can get us on the guest list for tonight's Baby Doll gig."

"Yay – that *is* good news!" agrees Sadie, "because Bell texted me earlier to say that the tix had sold out! She was freakin' out, my phone went off in the middle of class, and it was sooo embarr....Okay, forget it, so what can be so bad that your fizzog is arranged in such a glum, glum way, Lo-lo?"

"Eva has entered the Meet Tom Tootie contest too." I blurt out, no dramatic pauses, no nothing, it was cold hard fact.

"No way!" Sadie says. "This is going to need a whole lot of pink-thinkin', but we can't do that until we've stocked up..."

"Stocked up on what?" I ask.

She shows me the empty sweet wrapper, and says "Chocolate, of course."

Bella, who is rockin' a rather cute denim shorts and faded tee combo had gone into a mild hyperventilating state at the thought of not getting tix for tonight's gig, so she practically smothered Sadie and I in love and kisses when she met us after school.

"How much are we loving Jake right now?" she asks no one in particular.

"Well, as nice as he is to look at," I begin, "and as great as it that he's promised to get us on tonight's guest list, we are not loving him a whole lot actually," I inform her before she starts getting a little too liberal with the Jake love. "His girlfriend Evil Eva, has entered the *Missy* competition too," I tell her

"And...?" Bella says expectantly, like she's waiting for the punchline or something.

"Well, that's it, but that's bad enough..." I don't think Bella's sensing the severity of the situation.

"Well, only if you actually care, Lola Love," she says, putting her long tanned arm around my shoulder as we walk along the beach towards home. I can sense one of those older and wiser moments coming on.

"Lo, loads of people will enter, but we put together a killer package and we're good, we're The Rainbow Hearts and we rock and rule, remember?" she says. "Come with me," she hollers as she races across the pebbles down towards the sea. Sadie and I look at each other, join hands and run to the waters edge to join her.

"Okay, so pick up a pebble," Bella instructs us when we finally reach her all out of breath and wind swept by the salty sea air. I pick a big smooth stone while Sadie opts for a rough looking tiny one and we hold them in our hand waiting for our next instruction.

"So Lo, I think you worry far too much about Eva, and if you let her, she'll eat you up inside. She may be an awful person but that's her stuff, not yours, 'k?" Why does all the good self-help stuff sound so much better when an American-o says it?

I do let Eva bother me, I know that, and it's a huge deal that no matter what I do, it's like she's always there y'know? But I've got a new 'tude, great mates and Bell's right, Evil might have a band, but The Rainbow Hearts, rock and rule.

"Now take your pebbles, ladies," Bella informs us, "channel any sucky not-nice energy into the pebble and throw it, throw it into the sea and let it wash away with the tide."

Sadie took next to no time as she hardly suffers sucky feelings ever, but I put all the badness I felt when I thought of Eva into the pebble, and I threw it, as hard as I could, into the sea. Ahhhhhhhh, insta-calm. It was a moment of total zenification, Bella was not only a guitar-goddess she was also, courtesy of yoga dad, a zen queen too.

"Now, come on you two," Bella says already making her way back up over the pebbles to the promenade, "we've got a gig to go to, race you home!"

Chapter twelve

Baby Doll are a local band who have made it big, as in really big. They haven't forgot where they came from though, and play at The Ballroom on The Pier regularly and tickets usually sell out within an hour of going on sale.

I say all this like I actually know what I'm talking about, but Bella has given me the Baby Doll 101 and has downloaded their back catalogue on my iPod, I'm not exactly sure of their 'sound' or whatever it is you say when referring to music types, but according to Bella, they are what's known as mod-rock-cool. After listening to a few songs while getting ready, I think I like mod-rock-cool.

"Well, what do you say LL?" Bella asks twisting and turning, she's working a look not too dissimilar to the lead singer of Baby Doll herself, in head-to-toe black with splashes of yellow in the form of beads and pin badges, she looked mysterious and classic, in a fresh and bold way. The only difference is Cody Silk has a short black bob, and Bell has flowing platinum blonde locks borrowed from a movie star siren from yesteryear but she rocks them in a way that is altogether Bella-tastic.

Sadie has agreed to meet us there as she was getting a lift

with her bro, so once I had put on my candy-stripe neck scarf and pink shirt dress, cinched in at the waist with a silver belt, Bella and I were good-to-go girls about town. I shout to ma-parental that I'll be home by 9.30, ma-parental shouts back "9.30 or I'll be calling the police, now go have a nice night!"

I shake my head in despair, as I shut the door behind me.

Under the flashing light bulbs that spelt out 'welcome to the pier' in bright, fluro-colours, there were an assortment of our seaside town's hipster-cools queuing the pier's entire length and bustling with excitement. Taking me firmly by the hand, Bella and I walk tall, past the people trying to sell-over priced tickets that might not even be real, safe in the knowledge that we were on the guest list. I must say, it did feel really rather fab, striding past the cool-clad hipsters like we're making our way down a catwalk, a few mutter 'who are they?' I want to tell them that we're The Rainbow Hearts actually, and we rock and rule, but now wasn't the time for publicising our band, we had a some guitar-girl learning to do.

Watching Bella in action is like watching re-runs of old classics. Flutterby lashes and a sweet-as-sugar smile get us past the bouncers, no questions asked, and we are directed towards a familiar looking girl with a clipboard. She's chewing gum as if her life depends on it.

"Hey there, we're on the list," Bella informs the clipboard queen, reaching across to see if she can find our names.

"What are your names?" The girl asks snatching the board away from Bella and pulling it close to her chest. Some people take their jobs way too seriously.

"Bella and Lola" I reply. "Lola Love."

The girl, who I really thought I recognised but still couldn't place, looked me up and down and without even checking her board, snapped, "Sorry, you're not on the list!"

"But you haven't even looked!" screeched Bella.

The girl ignores Bella, which is a skill in itself because one thing Bella is not, is the kind of girl you ignore, and she moves on to the boys with slicked back hair behind us.

Back outside the venue we are undeterred. We are Pink Ladies after all. Bella and I plan ways in which we could get inside, and it is clear that we are mucho creative girls, because our suggestions get more ridiculous each time around.

"We could go round to the back door and say we're backing singers for Baby Doll" I begin.

"Or" suggests Bella, "we could think action sequence, we could get our manga girl fabulousness on and kick bouncer bee-hind!"

"Or" I add, "we could avoid the bouncers entirely by developing spidey-girl skills, and swing above their heads, wrap them in a sticky goo, land upside down on the ceiling, stay really still, when everyone is inside, ditch the blue and red costume – because even I know that's a fashion faux pas – and walk casually inside like we'd been there all along – what d'ya think?"

"I think you're as funny as pink fluff, Li-Lo," she says ruffling my pink 'do as we sit on the pier railings, dangling our legs and kicking our heels. Bella was no longer feeling the love for Jake, and right this minute, neither was I.

"I can't understand it," I say trying to fathom why Jake would say one thing and do another. I was finding it really hard to think bad thoughts about him. "Jake said he knew the person on the door and that he'd put us on the guest list." My Nancy Drew detective skills were officially defunct.

"Boys, LL-cool-girl, can not be trusted," says Bella. "It's a real life, actual fact."

I nod in agreement. That's why Tom Tootie, celeb boy swoonster, was a far better and more superior choice of crush. "Pah to real life stinky Jake Farrell," I say, kicking my foot so hard that my pink pump comes off.

"Ahhh, allow me *mademoiselle*," Ooh-la-la Frenchville Charlie is like a modern day prince charming, appearing from right outta nowhere to remind Bella and I that not *all* boys are bad. He bends down and pops my pink pump back on my foot.

"Why, thank you kind sir!" I say jumping to my feet.

"Why are you bee-yoouuu-tiful ladiez not inside making giggy-giggy dance movez?" Charlie asks.

"Because someone, mentioning no names...Jake Farrell," I cough, "was supposed to put us on the guest list, but didn't."

"That is weirdo," Charlie says looking confused, he knows Jake and like me, can't understand why he wouldn't be a boy of his word.

But Charlie is *absolutment* a boy of his word and has a boy-pal on the concession stand, who when texted, let Bella and I slip in unnoticed behind Charlie. It wasn't quite the movie-star entrance I would have hoped for, but the end result was the same.

We were in.

Chapter thirteen

The 'how to be a guitar-playin' goddess girl' lessons start right here, inside The Ballroom.

This is like no classroom I've ever been in. It has glitterballs for a start. Now, I like glitterballs a lot, but a glitterballs alone, does not a great venue make. If I'm honest, The Ballroom is a bit of a dive, but it has earned itself a reputation for being *the* place to hear cool music.

I didn't think Bella was expecting me to take notes, this was much more of a hand-on kinda assignment, but an IM to self: don't wear pretty things at a gig, because the heat of the room is wrapping itself around me and making my dress feel a li'l too snug and my cute, pink pumps are sticking to the carpet. Ick.

This is not the most perfect of Lola locales, but, as the pink thinkin' rules state, a pink thinking chica must always swap a Negative Nina Thought for one of Pink Positivity – so while the locale may lack prettiness and general loveliness, it is made 100 times better by Ooh-la-la Charlie. Who, for the record, could not be any cuter if he was able to stand on his hands and hula-hoop all at the same time. He has bought me a pink lemonade and has even got the bar dude to put in a cherry on a stick – very NYC

– my aunt Lullah, would be proud.

Charlie and I chink glasses and exchange grins. I've never had a boy-pal before, it was really rather cool.

"Li-Lo, they're going to be on any second, come on!" Bella shouts to be heard above a band called The Raven Rascals. They have a huge following who all wear thick, black eyeliner like the lead singer, Raven, even the boys. Bella bear hugs me from behind, I take a sip of my lemonade, pass the glass to Charlie and we pogo to the front of the crowd.

This is Bella in her natural surroundings, and she is one very happy version of herself. Guitars, and girls who play guitars, are Bella's passion and when someone is passionate about something, they shine like a neon pink sign. That was Bella right now.

It's only when the sounds of the crowd reach a deafening pitch that Baby Doll make their entrance. Bella, still hugging me tight, screams loud in my ear as lead singer, Aubrey takes to the stage. She is dressed in a grey Mickey Mouse top that has been customised into a vest and a red chiffon dip-dyed skirt that had also been unable to escape the scissors. Her sharp, black bob had been replaced with auburn curls that spill onto her shoulders, wigs really are the coolest accessory – and an oversized pair of red-rimmed sunglasses cover half her face.

She counts in "...1, 2, 3, 4" and goes straight into a song about dreaming big dreams. She was coolio-a-go-go. I could see why Bella thinks she rocks. Bella knows all the words and she sings them all in my ear as we jump and scream and clap and cheer. This is the best assignment ever, and as taking real notes in a mosh pit is really not convenient, I'm taking mental notes, it's a journo-girl, y'know.

Things that make Baby Doll awesome:

Stage presence
Star quality
And being really, really nice to their fans

Some celeb-girls think they have to be rude and cuss a lot to be cool, I bet that's what Evil Eva's band will do, but Baby Doll just rock out, have a good time and make really, really good music. Personally, I think that's a million gazillion times cooler.

"Finally, I've found you!"

Sadie has worked her way through the pogo-ing crowd. We'd been looking for her earlier, but Bella had just assumed she was hangin' with her bro. Bella and Sadie's bro, Scott have 'history' so we didn't look too hard to try and find them. "Charlie said you'd been kidnapped by a jump-jump Bell," Sadie hollers above the screechy guitar, "so I knew you'd be near the front! I was worried that you wouldn't be able to get in, what with Eva's sister on the door," Sadie shouts in my ear.

"What?" I ask, "the li'l miss 'tude with a clipboard is Evil Eva's sister?"

Sadie nods to confirm. Well, that would make a whole lot of sense. They were obviously cut from the same bad-girl cloth. Which, maybe, just maybe, meant Jake wasn't so awful after all. Seriously though, boys are really pretty to look at but they're not girls, and girls, well, girls that *aren't* Eva, are the very best.

My ears are ringing, I have been pogo-ing with Bell and Sade for half an hour – pogo-ing is my new favourite exercise, f'sure – and I don't think I've ever had quite so much fun.

I wish Angel was here, though. Although, if I know Angel, which I think I do after 14 years, this would not have made her love the rockage, this would have given her a million zillion reasons not to be in a band, EVAH. And that would be the worst, because The Rainbow Hearts were different – we were from

Girlsville, which was just a little way left of Serious-Rockington. In Girlsville, bands are formed through fun and friendship and the music is just a really rather fabulous extra. Sssh, don't tell Bella that though, she'd totally want to be a resident of Serious-Rockington.

While there was a good chance my shirt dress wasn't about to turn to rags *a la* Cinders any time soon, but my watch is telling me that I have exactly 15 minutes to get home before the ma-parental would call the police, and my ma-parental? She's a woman of her word.

I tap on my watch in the direction of Bella, kiss Sadie on the cheek and despite trying to find Charlie to thank him for being our very own fairy godmother, we have to go. Bella and I negotiate rough terrain – a too-big barking dog and a prickly hedgerow – before arriving home with nanoseconds to spare.

I briefly thank Bell for our too-cool-for-school evening of rock with a hug and a mock 'rock' sign and put the key in the door. I check my watch, 9.32. Dang it. The parental was going to do head spins, I know it.

Now, I'm a pink positive thinker, but the sitch-u that was set out before me was sky-rocketing even off of my positivity radar.

"Oh, hey Lola," ma-parental says looking up from her rather comfy looking spot on the sofa. She's sat really close to yoga-dad, and she's not even attempting to move and pretend to be coy and apologetic. In fact, she was anything but. Even Cat had ditched her 'tude, although I think that's something to do with yoga-dad working his zen magic on her. She is twisting herself around my legs and as I stroke her, the hissy, not-nice noise she usually makes, has been replaced with a real cat purr.

"Is that the time already?" mum asks looking at her non-existent watch. "Time just flies when you're having fun, doesn't it?" she says, giving yoga-dad a friendly nudge. He smiles really wide and they look like they're having...well, fun.

And that wasn't even the best bit, No, the best bit was that yoga dad and mum were eating sushi. There was a time, in the not so long ago past, that my ma-parental wouldn't have even known what sushi was, let alone entertained the idea of actually eating it.

This was pink-tinted progress. I still had a long way to go before ma-parental was a fully-embracing, signed-up, pink-thinking Pink Lady, but she was proof that letting the niceness in (and yoga-dad is niceness personified) can make life really rather sweet, which is one small step for ma, and one giant leap for pink-thinking. Yay!

Chapter fourteen

The Rainbow Hearts tips for success

Create a mantra/affirmation: ours is 'The Rainbow Hearts rock and rule' and repeat at least three times a day, as a reminder of who you are and what you want to be!

See it to believe it: Mentally rehearse an event or see yourself as superstar confident and play it like a movie in your mind. Imagine all the things you want to happen, happening and keep playing it over and over until you create a permanent hard copy of success that is uploaded to your brain's computer.

Nothing beats real-life actual practising: you don't get good at what you do without practice. That's factuality.

The past two weeks have seen us sticking to our Rainbow Hearts tips for success like glue. We've been visualising, we've been repeating our affirmation and we've also had real actual band practices. Well me, Bell and Sadie have, and Angel has joined us at the weekends. Although, Angel is far more worried about how she looks than how she actually sounds, which makes Sadie and I laugh, but makes Bella sigh out loud and tsk tsk like an adult, a lot. Now, more than ever, I totally and utterly believe that The Rainbow Hearts are going to rock and rule and win the *Missy* contest.

Which is why, right now as I look at the envelope that has just arrived, with a *Missy* magazine logo on the front, I do a happy shape-throwing dance in the style of a tippy-toe rhumba – it's a Lola creation ok? - before I even open it.

I toy momentarily with the idea of waiting for the others so that we can open it together, but that would mean waiting 'til the weekend for Angel to come home and I just wouldn't be able to leave a *Missy* magazine envelop un-opened. I just wouldn't. And what if the reply changed because we'd taken too long to open it? You just don't know what jiggery pokery goes on inside an un-opened envelope, and quite frankly I don't want to find out, so I rip it open.

Missy Magazine
Teen Towers
London
0207 307 4735

To The Rainbow Hearts – Lola, Bella, Sadie and
Angel

CONGRATULATIONS!

We loved your originality and your entry definitely
stood out from the rest, which is why we would
love to invite you to London, next week, to take part
in the Missy Magazine Battle of the Bands!
You will stay in a five star hotel (details enclosed)
and if you win, you and The Rainbow Hearts will
meet The Tootie after their performance.

Please ring the number above to confirm you'll be
attending and that an adult will be accompanying
you. All equipment will be provided – you provide
the entertainment!

Can't wait to meet you, Rainbow Hearts!

Tori Frankel
Editor

The tippity-toe rhumba has now turned into a crazy un-nameable move that involves; jumping up and down on the spot, 1980's style body-poppin' and lying on the floor kicking my legs in the air.

I am positively sing-songing with happiness.

We, The Rainbow Hearts - me, Sadie and Bella were going to play in *Missy* magazine's Battle of The Bands. We were going to the big city of London, home of all things cool and Londonish. These things were certain. The letter said so.

We were also going to win and we were going to meet the cutie that is Tom Tootie. Except these things aren't altogether certain just yet, but they absolutely will be, just you wait and see – pink thinkin' rules like that.

Oh, and let's not forget, that as well as all this fabulousity, I have in my hands, a letter from Tori Frankel, editor of *Missy* magazine. It's signed and everything. If I'm not mistaken, this could quite possibly be the happiest day of my life ever.

Bella has Joan Jett, Angel has *tres* cool fashion designer Anna Sui, Sadie has chick with sticks Meg White, and I, Lola Love have Tori – short for Victoria, y'know – Frankel. Tori is a total real-life inspir-o girl. I love Audrey and Marilyn and all, but what with them not being around anymore, I'm very limited as to the life lessons I can learn from them, Tori is totally living the dream. She's only 26 and she's the youngest ever magazine editor in the UK. I did a project on her for English and found out loads of cool stuff about her, she has a pug dog called Walter for a start. Have you seen how adorably cute those dogs are? Sssshh, don't tell Cat, but I would trade her in any day for my very own pug dog.

She did work experience for *So Very Now* magazine, and survived (FYI *So Very Now* is a super swank magazine with an editor who has a reputation that would completely rival Miranda

Priestley's in the movie *The Devil Wears Prada*) and, the most inspir-o thing ever, is that she got her first job on a glossy magazine by sending lots of editors photocopied pages from her very own zine – yep, she was a zine queen, just like me!

She rocks. A lot.

I'm still doing the un-named dance of joy when ma-parental passes by my boudoir door. She would normally shake her head in bemusement and mutter something under her breath about how I take after my Aunt Lullah or something like that, but she doesn't. She just smiles, it's still awkward looking and not quite teeth-bearing yet, but hey, I guess smiling for the ma-parental is like guitar-playing for me, something we'll both get better at with practice.

"What's going on, Lola Love?" she asks.

"We've done it, we're through to the Battle of the Bands!" I tell her, before remembering I've not actually told her about the Battle of the Bands – what if she doesn't let me go?

"Battle of the what?"

"So," I begin carefully, "there was this competition in *Missy* magazine, y'know, the magazine I really like?" I check her face for recognition and there's definitely movement, I'd even go as far to say it was a nod. "Well anyway," I continue, a girl's got to work with what she's got, "there was this competition, we had to send a demo, and now we've won a place in The Battle of the Bands, which is just so exciting!" I take a breath and not knowing how this one was going to go, I cross my fingers behind my back. Y'know, just in case.

"Really?" Ma-parental says, "Well done Lola, where's it going to be held? In town?"

Okay, so here's where a plan of action would of come in really handy, because even though the big city of Londinium was literally only a 40 minutes train ride away, it might as well be in blimmin' Antartica as far as the ma-parental was concerned. She didn't like it. She didn't like anywhere that wasn't Dullsville-by-sea.

"No, it's in London," I say under my breath, hoping that if I say it quieter it might make it okay.

"London?" she repeats, "oh, I don't think so, Lola Love, do you?" While it might sound like she was asking me a question, believe me, if you could hear her tone you'd know that it was very much a statement of factuality. And, just in case I was in any doubt whatsoever as to whether that was the end of the matter, she turns on her heel and makes her way back down the stairs.

I knew it was too good to be true. I knew that the ma-parental couldn't keep up this act o' nice indefinitely, thing is, I didn't want to be right. I wanted to be wrong, because I was growing to very much like the mark two ma-parental.

I take a deep yoga breath. Breathe in for five, hold, breathe out for five. Bella taught me to do deep breaths in times of all things messy and stressy. This was deffo one of those times. Why would ma-parental purposely want me to miss out on the best thing that was going to happen to me ever? It's like she purposely wants to ruin anything remotely pink-tinted in my life. Oh, wait a minute, she does.

Just short of stomping my foot and screaming 'that's not fair' like every teen girl drama queen before me, I hear the whoop, whoop sound of my internal pity party alarm. A bum-kick to remind me that this was the stuff of my pink-tinted dreams and that giving in was not an option. There was simply no way this leading lady's movie wasn't going to have a happy ending. I mean, she hadn't said no yet, had she?

And, in the nanoseconds I'd assessed the situation, I realise

I've got a secret weapon.

Chapter fifteen

"Bell, yoga dad has got to help us, she said I can't go and I've got to go, he's got to persuade the ma-parental to let me go to London, he's the only one she'll listen to and..."

Bella holds up her hand in front of my face and stops me mid-rant. "Chica, chill," she says in this soothing Californian tone that doesn't sound like it belongs to the same person who sings all those raspy bad-girl pop-rock-punk tunes.

"Now what's the hurry, Miss McFlurry?" she asks passing me a cup of peppermint tea. "Blow," she instructs before I can answer, "it's hot, just like your head, now breathe." She sits cross-legged in front of me and tells me to repeat after her, "in with love out with hate, in with love out with hate."

Welcome to the den of Zen.

I do what Bella asks and momentarily, I feel a wave of calm wash over me, I take a sip of tea and the hotness on my tongue sends a shockwave reminder that I'm not here to chillax, I was a girl on a mission. "Look Bella, this is really important – can we do the chillin' later when we've dealt with the craziness that is the ma-parental please?" I ask, putting the mug beside me on the floor.

Of course, Bella completely disagrees with my order of proceedings. She's like Yoda from *Star Wars*, 'cept she's not wrinkly, 3ft and green, and says things like "Lo, if we all took things a little slower, we'd get things done much, much quicker."

"Okay, okay," I say holding my hands up in surrender, "but Bell, you don't wanna do Battle of the Bands as a three-piece do you?" I ask.

"Why, what's happened?" she asks.

"Well, I got a letter from Missy Magazine..." I say.

"You did? What did it say?" she sits to attention and shuffles on her bum towards me. I take the letter from my Sadie-made tote – it's pink, natch, and has cute pin badges with slogans that Sadie has made specifically for me, like 'pretty in print' and 'zine queen' – and pass it to Bella. She takes a moment to skim read the important info and lets out a li'l totally un-Bella like yelp of happiness.

"Shut up! This is crazy-cool – have you told Sades and Angel yet?" she asks jumping to her feet and reaching for her mobile.

"No, I haven't," I tell her, fiddling with the badge on my bag, "because before I got a chance, the ma-parental turned mechanical menace and threw a huge-ass spanner in the works." I tell her.

"And she did that how?..." Bella asks, in a tone that almost can't believe it. Bella is a fan of the ma-parental.

"When I told her that Battle of the Bands was in London, she said 'I don't think so Lola Love, do you?' in that infuriating I-know-best tone and that was it. End of conversation."

Bella pulls her knees to her chest and picks at the black nail varnish on her toes. Bella's thinking. She always picks at nail varnish when she's thinking.

"So, she didn't actually say 'no' then?" asks Bella mid-pick.

"No," I confirm trying to remain optimistic, "but she did this whole turning around and walking away thing which is a sure sign that the subject it's non-negotiable. We NEED to get yoga dad to talk to her Bell, and if she still doesn't agree after that, he must know some hypnotic magic that will make her say yes, right?!"

Bell, clearly impressed at my solution-based thinking, gets to her feet and holds out her hand to pull me to mine.

"Lo, why do you think your mum's so protective?"

"Protective? She isn't protective, she's just annoying," I say.

"D'ya wanna know what I think?" asks Bella, she was going to tell me anyway so I didn't bother responding, "I think she doesn't like the thought of you leaving, because she's scared you might not come back, you know, like your dad..."

Bella's words were a little tiny bit like a punch to the stomach. It's funny how people who aren't actually living your life can take a look in from the outside and y'know, get it. It's like Bella's watched a 30 second movie trailer and got the entire picture, while I'm starring in the movie and don't even know the plotline.

"I guess I hadn't thought of it like that," I admit, because I hadn't, but while I'm now thinking of that, I'm not thinking of how to get my sweet self to Londinium. I'm all out of focus.

"Hey Lo, it says here," Bella says pointing to the *Missy* letter she was re-reading, "we need an adult to come with us, so let's go ask yog... my dad, if he'll come and, if he agrees, which I know he will, then your mum will definitely let us go. Don't worry Lo-Lo, The Rainbow hearts will go to the ball!"

So, getting picked for the Battle of the Bands – another tick on the Meet Tom Tootie to-do list. Hurrah!

Form a band ☑
Name the band ☑
Record a demo ☑
Get a look ☑
Practice ☑
Get picked ☑

Chapter sixteen

Yoga-dad is the go-go father of fabulousness. Fact.

Not only is he able to do crazy bendy poses, which is super impressive all on its own, not only did we not need to stoop to bribery to get him to agree to take us all to the Big City of Londinium, but most importantly of all, he was able to persuade my ma-parental that this was a once in a lifetime opportunity for me, and it'd be crazy to not to let me go. He didn't even have to do his whole southern Californian self-help talk on her either, I know this because Bella and I had been watching through the banister on the stairs, and when yoga-dad spoke, ma-parental did this funny thing with her mouth, like a lip quiver or something. Seriously he could have said 'eggs, chips and peas' and I think she would of agreed, and she hates eggs *and* chips *and* peas.

Anyway, the result of the lip quiver is that the Rainbow Hearts are a four-piece band, on a train, on the way to the Big City of Londinium. Go, yoga-dad. Luckily for us, he's one of those really cool parents who you don't mind hanging with either, he doesn't say mucho embarrassing things, he knows all about cool music, he even knows who The Tooties' are, he doesn't sing along to songs he doesn't know the words to, he's just a bendy, chillaxed parental of cool, who was taking us to Londinium, where we were going to win Battle of The Bands and we were going to meet Tom Tootie. It was a happy, happy day.

The girls and I bought yoga-dad a special book to say thank you, we went to a shop in The Lanes that sells pretty cushions, books and incense and decided to buy him a book about happiness with a picture of a monk on the front of it. Angel thought it was a bit silly, because he's by far the happiest person we know, but we all need li'l helpful reminders to keep doing the things we're good at, right? I mean, just because Bella is the best guitar player in the history of Girlsville, it doesn't mean she's going to stop getting good at it, does it?

And anyway, we wanted to tell him how happy he had made us, and we reckoned the monk book was a good way to do it. Bella said he'd love it, and what with him being her dad and all, we figured that was a good enough recommendation. She was right, he did love it, in fact, he's reading it right now. Angel is sat next to him applying lip-gloss and planning our individual looks for this afternoon's live show, Bella is plugged into her tunes and mouthing the words, and Sadie is knitting a cute li'l mp3 holder with pink sparkly wool. Personally, I'm finding it hard to sit still for longer than three minutes at a time as I'm filled-to-the-brim with excitement!

"Sade," I say nudging her with my elbow. "I wonder what the other band are going to be like?"

Sadie smiles, but doesn't look up from her knitting. "How funny would it be if it was Evil Eva and the Negative Ninas?"

I shudder, just thinking about it. "Er... I can't believe that you just went there, Miss Sadie," I say in a mock-American-Bella accent, "let me count the ways that *wouldn't* be funny!"

Ohmystars, that really wouldn't be funny, that would be the worse x 100.

"It really doesn't matter Lo-lo," Angel says looking up from her show notes, "because whoever we're up against we'll thrash them, we'll wipe the floor with them!" Angel really had developed a competitive streak at that swanksville boarding school and that, combined with her built-in head-sway 'tude, made her one sassy force to be reckoned with.

Yoga-dad looked up from his book, smirked, shook his head and went back to the line he was reading. Yet another reason why yoga-dad is cool. Other parentals would have said things like: 'Angel, it's the taking part, not the winning that matters' or 'Angel, that's not a very grown-up attitude now, is it? 'cept he didn't, it's like he always knows what's really going on yet he hardly ever says a word.

Sadie pulls out a picture of Tom Tootie that she wants signed and lets out a deep long sigh. "Lo, you do know that if all goes to plan, I may not be coming back with you tomorrow, don't you?" Sadie says stroking the poster, "when Tootie Cuti meets me, he'll want me to become his crafting, drum-playing girlfriend, and it would be really rude of me to turn him down, and you know I'm not rude, don't you? So I'm going to say yes, it's the right thing to do."

I laugh at Sadie. "Well, when Tom Cuti-Pa-Tootie realises I'm a writer-girl," I say, "he'll ask me to write the tour diaries which will mean having to skip school while I travel the world, but again, it would be rude not to, it's career development and everything!"

Angel shakes her head at us both and signals for Sadie to pass her the poster. "Let's take a look at this object of swoon then," she demands. Sadie begrudgingly hands over her poster. "This is the guy we're winning the Battle of the Bands for? Girls,

I'm sorry, but he's not all that and a bag of chips, is he?"

I can't believe she actually went there, but she did. She went to the place that no one else would dare, she went to diss-Tom-Tootie-ville, a dark place that people rarely visit, well not when Sadie and I are around anyway, but Angel who teeters on the edge of sassy on a near daily basis, just went there, one expensive designer shoe after the other.

"Angel Trueman," I say in my best mock-mad voice, "as I have know you the longest, I think it's only right that I let you know, that where you just went, is not a place that we go."

Angel's smirk said it all. She loves nothing more than creating a dramarama and will say anything for affect.

"I know what you're doing," I tell her, linking arms with Sadie, "but Sades and I are united in our Tom Tootie love and will not rise to your rudeness Miss Angel, anyway, Sades and I will happily leave you and Bella at the hotel tonight if you're not going to treat him with the guitar-boy love he deserves!"

Sadie claps with approval at my declaration of Too-cute Tootie support.

While Angel smiles and nudges Bella, "Did you hear that? They're threatening to leave us behind tonight while they go meet this poor imitation Johnny Depp!" Angel says pointing to Sadie's poster.

Bella pulls an earphone from her ear and hits the pause button. "Don't worry," Bella says putting her arm round Angel, "they can't go anywhere without my pops, right pops?" she says trying to get yoga-dad's attention by prodding him with her kicked-in Converse. He looks back up from his book, gives Bella a look that says a million words, seriously, he talks louder than anyone I know without words and then breaks into a killer-watt smile. He has a lovely smile, not a pulled-tight forced one, but a real, genuine one that made you feel really important when he shot one in your direction.

Bella was really lucky to have such a cool dad. Mine wouldn't have brought us to the Big City of Londinium, he could barely get off the sofa, in fact, he was so lazy it was a wonder he was able to actually leave us at all.

Bella interrupted my thoughts with tales of how she'd teach Tom Tootie and his brother James how to play guitar. "It's not that I don't like them," she says, "I just think they've got a lot to learn, y'know. They are boys after all!" We all laugh out loud, because no matter how much of a cutie-patooti Tom Tootie actually is, she was right.

"Exactly!" Angel laughs agreeing with Bella, "which is why, if I *have* to go, I would offer up some of my super-stylin' tips to them, because jeez, do they need it. I mean girls, are you seriously telling me you find those limp locks attractive?'

"Yes, yes, yes!" Sadie and I say in unison.

Bella and Angel shake their heads and before they can put together a case against why our object of swoon was not actually an object of soon after all, which, would have taken them a whole trip around the world twice, because it's absolutely, positively, not do-able, we've arrived. The Rainbow Hearts are in the Big City of Londinium.

Chapter seventeen

You wouldn't think the Big City of Londinium was only a 40 minute train journey from Dullsville-by-Sea, because when you get here, it seems like a million trillion miles away. It's not glam in the same way that New York or Paris are, but it's still unbelievably cool.

Yoga-dad knows London really well; he has famous client types who pay him to come to their big posh pile of bricks in places like Notting Hill and Bayswater just for an hour yoga session, that's crazy, isn't it? Still, his knowledge of all things Londinium means we have our very own tour guide and because it's a nice day and we're a little early, yoga dad suggests that we take a stroll to the river.

The second you step out of the olden days train station you can see the Millenium Eye and the Houses of Parliament, it's true, the Big City of Londinium is the biggest ever reminder that there is a whole wide world outside of Dullsville-by-Sea and it makes my belly flip with excitement. Here I was with three of the coolest gal-pals in the history of girl oh, and yoga-dad obv, about to take part in a Battle of the Bands competition and if, no, *when* we win, we were going to meet Tom Tootie. That just wouldn't have happened to the pre-think Pink Lola Love, in a crazy life-split type moment, I see myself still working a borin' snorin' hair do, having negative thoughts, no friends and throwing a full-blown, life long pity party – ick.

I shake my pink hair to get rid of any un-pink thoughts and just like when you shake a snow globe, the head shake creates an internal pink glitter storm and I smile with total happiness at my sweet-as-sugar life. I pass my camera to yoga-dad, ask him to make like a tourist and take snaps of the Rainbow Hearts in various tourist-y positions.

Bella, who has travelled all over the world with yoga-dad, is just not feeling the Big City of Londinium as much as the rest of us. While we're pointing out things we've seen in films, places we'll eat when we're famous and scratching our pretend beards as we discuss arty sculptures, Bella is keen to get to the Battle of the Bands venue and be a serious muso-girl and as much as I'm loving being a tourist, I too love being a muso-girl more.

"Pops," she asks, "this is great and all but can we just get going already? I need to get used to the new guitar, we need to check out the venue, and Angel needs to practice."

"I do?" Angel exclaims, putting her hand on her hip and pulling a pout that would rival any model-type. "I'll have you know, I'm the most amazing freak-out fabulous tam-tam player ever!"

Bella laughs "Of that, Angel Cakes, I have no doubt, we just all need to get our practice on together, that's all!"

"Okay, girls," yoga-dad says scooping us up in what feels like a bubble of total oasis-like calm amongst the bustle of tourists and Londinium people in busy-people suits rushing around like they're really rather busy, "lets jump in a taxi, drop our things at the hotel, and then we can go to the venue."

Wow, yoga-dad was good at quick-thinking plan making too. If there was an award for coolio-a-go-go adult, he would deffo get it.

The ride in the taxi made us feel like what celeb-girls must feel like when they're whisked from one really cool locale to another. The driver went really fast through places that we kept recognising from the TV and we were at the super-swanky hotel, paid for by the magazine – how cool is that? – in no time. It had shiny marble floors and comfy lose-yourself-in-them chairs in the lobby, and while yoga-dad checked us in, we continued to rock our celeb-girl fantasy and pretended we were doing an interview for *Missy* magazine.

"So, Bella," I ask holding out a rolled up magazine as a microphone, "you've won the battle of the bands, how do you feel?"

"Well, it was a hard run race," she says flicking her white-blonde hair over her shoulder, "but c'mon, we were really rather good, weren't we?"

We all laugh so loud that we cause an old lady wearing a tweed suit (ick) to pull her glasses down her nose and see what all the fuss is about. Sigh, it's The Rainbow Hearts, of course! Yoga dad waves a key fob to signal we're ready to go and we jump in the lift. It's a really glitzy, glam-tastic lift with far too much gold trim for my personal taste, but rich people love gold, that's why posh places have so much of it.

Our room was no different. It was huge with gold trim everywhere, even the toilet seat. I don't think it's real gold, well I hope not, because that would just be wasteful when there were poor people in the world. Bella and Sadie are already jumping on the bed and Angel is quick to join them, I throw my overnight bag to the floor and dive bomb the bed too.

"I'll give you girls a half hour," yoga-dad says, "I'll just be next door if you need me!"

If this is what being a real life celeb girl is like, then I think I could really get used to it. Hanging with my gal-pals, jumping on beds in rooms with too much gold, having complimentary bags of M&Ms on each pillow and silly amount of channels on the TV. Happy days!

"Er... girls, a half hour is practically no hour," says Bella in her most worried tone, "we've got to get our glam girl on, NOW!"

The room soon became a whirly blur of make up, hairspray, perfume and flying items of clothing, we had the music channel on loud while we got ready and just as Angel was applying 'sorbet pink' lip gloss to my pre-pout lips, The Tootie come on the TV screen and we all scream, even super-cool Bella, and Sadie and I get to our feet, wiggle our hips and sing all the words to their last song, 'Girl is Supernatural' at the top of our voices.

"Er... girlies, ten minutes," Angel says tapping her plastic red watch as the song finishes, "there is no time for frivolity!"

Sadie and I salute Angel as we make the finishing touches to what will later be termed on the pages of magazines as The Rainbow Hearts look (even if it's only my zine).

So, in order of appearance, Super Sadie has emphasised her impish charm in a customised ensemble. She has hand printed a pink 'I heart Donnie Darko' tee and teamed it with a pink neck scarf. She's been quite the design-o girl and produced a cutting edge, cut-off denim skirt with cute apple patches on the pockets and paired it with the most fabulous pair of pink cowboy boots – yee-haah. Next up is Angel with attitude, who has a cute, flirty, take-me-to-the-ball dress in bright red with a pink ribbon tied under her ladybumps. Beauty*Licious Bella, the ultimate punk princess, finally decided after a total of four costume changes that involved switching from vampish diva to kitsch thrift queen to rock chick, that she would opt for high-octane 1920s glam. Her lacy dress is complimented with a smokey grey eyeshadow, several coats of black, black, black mascara and lashings of berry lip-gloss. On some people it would look too much, on Bella, it looks completely punk princess fierce. Last but by no means least, me Lola Love is working the dress of my dreams, a baby pink, strapless, 50s style prom dress with lots of underneath netting to make it twist and twirl, worn with super-cute ballet pump. And, ahem, my tiara. I had everything crossed that Angel would be too excited to notice.

It was official. We were gorgeous and glam-like.

Fact.

In a waft of pink perfumed girliness we leave the hotel and make our way to the venue.

"I wonder if we'll get a dressing room?" Sadie asks. "Maybe we'll have to share with the other band? I wonder if they're a guitar band too? Maybe they'll be goth-rock, what if they're emo-pop? Ohhh, I'm so excited!"

"Really?" says Bella sarcastically, she has gotten really good at that since being in the UK, "I'd never have guessed!"

As we turn the corner onto a main road, a Londinium taxi beeps it horn at us, demanding our attention. A girl-shaped blur shouts out the window but the taxi is going way to fast to hear what they were actually saying. Yoga-dad says this is normal behaviour in the Londinium and that he has to take a lot deeper breaths than usual when he comes here.

Undeterred by neither Bella's sarcasm nor the pesky noisy traffic, Sadie continues. "Well I *am* excited! I'm all filled up with the anticipation of it all, aren't you?" Sadie asks, looking for back up.

"Oh, I'm not," says Angel, "sure, I'm looking forward to it, who doesn't love to be the centre of attention? But I'm not nervy, not at all, it'll be a breeze – bring it on!"

"Wow, I wish I had your confidence, Angel!" I tell her, "I'm..." I pause mid-sentence because it doesn't matter what I was previously, which FYI: was mildly nervous and very excited, I am now petrified. This place is funk-da-mazingly huge. I tap Angel's arm and try to say words like 'wow' and 'blimey' but nothing comes out.

We're all standing in the road, open-mouthed at the sheer bigness of it all, when the taxi that had just passed with the shouty blur girl, pulls up alongside us, winds down his window, and in the direction of yoga-dad says, "'Ere mate, I hope you know what you're letting yourself in for, those girls I just had in the back of 'ere? Blimmin' nightmare, they were!"

Yoga-dad gives him a li'l nod and the guy rolls his eyes to the sky in a 'don't-say-I-didn't-warn-you' kind of way before driving off at top speed. Can you imagine The Rainbow Hearts being a diva, diva nightmare? Never!

Chapter eighteen

Okay, so here's the deal.

Today is much bigger than we'd expected. In fact, take how big we actually thought it was and times it by a million trillion and then you'll be somewhere close. I have been so caught up in the meet Tom Tootie-ness of it all that I didn't actually realise Battle of the Bands was part of a proper, honest to hotness Tootie gig, where lots of people, make that hundreds of people, would come along and pay to see The Tootie play all properly.

Woah.

We make our way to the venue doors and there are already girls outside queuing. Some girls have two T's written on their cheeks in black kohl eyeliner in homage to their fave guitar boys. One of them, a girl with lots of red bouncy curls, comes up to barriers and says in a speed that would rival a racing car driver, "Who are you? Do you know The Tootie? Are you their girlfriends? Can you get us backstage?"

This girl thinks we're famous, she even thought we might be The Tootie's girlfriends. We all look at each other, turn away for a nanosecond do a silent squeal of joy and come back to the curly-haired girl of fabulousness.

"We're the Rainbow Hearts," I say taking on my un-official role as the band's spokesgirl, "we've won a place in the Battle of the Band competition, will you vote for us?!!"

"You're much nicer than the other group," the red-headed girl smiled, "they've just gone through and were all like, 'we're far too good to speak to you' and they said they knew Tom Tootie and that they were going to hang out with him."

Jeez, how could they be rude to people when they weren't even a real band yet?

"Ohh, I don't know about that," I tell the girl, "but we can't get you in, 'coz look, we can't even get in ourselves right now!" Bella and Angel were trying the handles on the door with no luck. While Sadie and I chat to a few of the girls about The Tootie, Yoga-dad rings the number of the Missy contact we've been given and in seconds, this really adorable looking blonde-haired girl with a clipboard and Madonna-style headset came to the door to greet us.

"Hey ladies, I'm Caitlin," she shouts, "you must be The Rainbow Hearts!" and plants a kiss on each of our cheeks, so showbiz, she shakes yoga-dad's hand, and I don't know why, but she did a li'l lip quiver thing, just like ma-parental, when he spoke to her too – weird.

I wave to the red head and tell her to enjoy the show and she waves back shouting, "I'm Lisa by the way, and I'll be voting for The Rainbow Hearts!"

"So, are you girls super-excited?" Caitlin asks. She has his really high-pitch enthusiastic tone that is really infectious.

"Absolutely," I tell her, walking in double steps to walk beside her as we make our way through the backstage corridors. "So," I ask, "do you work for Missy magazine?"

"I do!" she says shooting me a smile.

"What's it like?" I ask, "it's just I want to be a journo-girl, well I am a journo-girl, because I write my own 'zine but I would love to work at *Missy*!"

"That's so cool that you write your own zine, did you bring one with you?" Caitlin asks.

"I did! You wanna see?" I ask delving in my bag, not waiting for her to respond.

"Wow – it looks great, mind if I keep it?" she ask rolling it up and popping it in her back pocket.

"Sure," I say, "maybe you could pass it on to Tori Frankel, she's my absolute idol-girl!" I know it was a bit cheeky, but a journo-girl grabs every opportunity that she can, that's what Tori herself says, I read it and everything.

"I will, I promise," she says, "Tori is cool, working for Missy is the best job ever! I get to write, I get to meet cute popstars and I get to work at events like this – what's not to love?"

She was right, it did sound pretty perfect.

"Right, here you go Rainbow Hearts!" Caitlin shouts to the whole group. Bella has been walking arm-in-arm with yoga-dad and Angel was wiping a teeny bit of mascara from under Sadie's eye. We all stop and stare as we have our own room with a sign.

I know.

I ask yoga-dad to take a snap of us with our door sign and we shout "Rainbow Hearts, rock and rule" as he clicks the picture.

"Right ladies," Caitlin yells over all the backstage noise, "you're going to get 20 minute rehearsal time, in about ten minutes, ok?" we all silently nod at cute Caitlin in agreement.

"I'll come get you," she continues, "walk you down to the stage area, you can have a practice and then I'll bring you back here while we let the crowd in – and then Rainbow Hearts, it's showtime!"

We all do an out-loud squeal of joy and happiness.

"Caitlin," asks Sadie, "Erm... What are the other band like? Can we meet them?"

Caitlin's perma-smile turns to a slight frown as she points down the corridor, "Do you want me to introduce you? They're just down here," she says, leading us behind her. "It's really weird," Caitlin says as she knocks on the door, "because I think they come from the same town as you guys."

"Really?" I say trying to get a look at the door sign, There were lots of bands in our town, it was really well known for its music scene, so I bet Bell or Sadie will definitely know them, but the door opens before I can get a look at what they're called, and it turns out we *all* knew them.

Chapter nineteen

"What?" spits the familiar voice of Eva Satine from the other side of the door, "I was practicing my acceptance speech!"

Seriously, it's between us and them? Of all the people, in all of the whole entire world, why was Eva crashing my dream day? It's like she's got a hotline to my dreams and wishes and will stop at nothing to bring them crashing down.

"Oh, fancy seeing you here!" Eva says, grinning from ear to ear, all stretched out on a giant sofa. The rest of her 'band' were sat in the corner and didn't look half as confident as Evil Eva. But then no one was. "Try to enjoy your fifteen minutes of fame today, won't you? Because when you're heading back to the hotel we'll be kicking back with The Tooties'!"

"Well, you'd have to actually be good for that to happen, and since you're not, it's going to make life pur -retty difficult," Angel says mid-head sway.

"Now, now girls," interrupts Caitlin sounding slightly flustered, "lets get you back to your room."

"Toodle pip girlies!" says Eva blowing a kiss from the sofa.

"Y'know, I was only joking when I said our competition might be Eva and The Negative Ninas," says Sadie, pacing back and forth across our room.

"Look, lets not panic," says Bella being significantly grown up about the whole crazy sitch we currently found ourselves in. "They've only had Jake to help them practice, and while you might think he's cute to look at Lo, he's no rock-god, so I can't imagine they've got anything that comes close to The Rainbow Hearts!"

Bella had a habit of being right but they must be a little bit good to have got this far, mustn't they? I contemplate my own pity-party version of events and whilst tempting, that's just not the way this pink-thinking chica rolls anymore. Besides, we'd worked so hard at getting good for today, it would be rude and wrong to not go out there and completely rock out.

"Okay," I say, pulling myself to my feet, brushing down my dress and pulling on my Madonna-esque fingerless gloves, "there's really no point comparing ourselves to the competition, they're not us, we are and we're The Rainbow Hearts and we rock and rule, right?!"

"Right!" everyone says in unison as we all high-five, like the retro-lovin' pop princesses we are.

Caitlin pops her head round the door mid session. "So, you ready for your rehearsal, ladies?"

"Abso-blimmin'-lutely!" I say, grabbing my girls and following Caitlin to the stage.

Wowzers.

This was a real stage with rigging and lights and when you looked out, you couldn't see anything except blackness because the seats went back so far. This was ah-mazing, our time to shine, and there was no way, bo-jay, that Eva was going to spoil it. So what if this was our fifteen minutes of fame? It would be the best fifteen minutes in the whole wide world!

Bella picks up a guitar, passes it to me and fiddles with a few of the knobs on the speaker. I still know nothing about all the techno-malarky that makes the guitar sound like a real music-making machine, so Bella plugs me in and makes it happen, I strum at the strings and it echoes around the whole venue. Ohmystars!

Bella plugs in her own guitar, Sadie bashes at the drums and super-confident Angel is just staring out at the blackness.

"You okay Angel?" I ask as I fiddle with my strings.

"Y...y...yeah, why wouldn't it be?" She says. I don't know, but she didn't seem like my Angel. For sure, she looked cool as cool can be in her totally inappropriate for rocking out outfit, but she didn't seem to be loving it. Not one little bit.

"Okay girls, you ready?" Sadie and I nod, Angel hesitates and Bella counts us in, "a 1, a 1, a 1, 2, 3, 4..."

I love playing guitar. I love writing because it helps me express my thoughts and feelings but when you play guitar, you completely lose yourself in the moment and you just know that right there and then is all that matters, it's such a buzz.

Angel wasn't really playing in time but she looked awesome and Sadie was more than capable of making enough noise to cover up any mistakes and Bella sang with a raspy tone that was coated in yummy caramel. We really did rock and rule.

As Bella played the last note, a couple of claps came from the front row. It was two ladies, one of them I could see was Caitlin and the other, I couldn't quite make out, but I recognised her face. Bella and I did a li'l thank you bow and made our way off the stage.

"Lola, wait up," shouts Caitlin across the stage. I turn around and standing beside her is only the blimmin' editor of *Missy* magazine, Tori Frankel. I want to do that silent squeal of joy and happiness thing, but now is really not the time. Tori looks just like her picture on the inside front cover of the magazine, she is the most uber-glam-girl I have ever seen.

"Hi, I'm Tori," the glamazon lady says, holding her hand out. I really wanted to high-five her but I could see that wasn't appropriate either, so I shake her bejewelled hand and feel myself smiling at her inanely.

"You guys were so great! I love that you have a dancing tambourine girl – so cool!" I smile at her not knowing what to say. "Caitlin tells me you make zines, too?"

"Yes, yes I do" I say. I also want to tell her how amazing she is, how she's totally inspired me, along with Audrey Hepburn, Bella, Sadie and Angel obv, and how much I love Missy magazine, 'cept I don't, instead I just keep grinning at her until she tells me how much she's looking forward to getting a look at my zine and wishes me luck for the performance.

"You should come and do work experience with us some time," Tori smiles before disappearing backstage.

"Thank you," I shout after her as she leaves. She turns and gives me a li'l wave. I totally do the squeal of joy and happiness thing, I just can't help it.

Chapter twenty

"Maddie, they were good, really good, are you sure you can fix it so that we win?"

Er...What the funk?

So, I'm in the loo, trying to have five minutes happy-to-be-me breathing time when I inadvertently become an accessory to plotting. Worse still, it's Eva plotting. The very worse kind. I don't know who Maddie is, but I don't like the idea that she might be able to fix the competition so that Eva and The Nina's win. I'm holding my breath as I listen, but my heart is beating so fast with the pressure of not trying to move, I'm sure that they'll hear it.

Seriously though, Eva is not very good at plotting, because I've watched enough teen girl movies to know that you would totally check all the cubicles before talking about something you didn't want others to know. Then again, Eva's a li'l bit silly like that, actually she's a lot silly like that.

"Stop freaking out. I told you, I would sort it. Am I not the best cousin ever?" the person that isn't Eva says. My own detective girl skills have deduced that the other girl is called Maddie and she is in fact Eva's cousin. I know, just call me Nancy Drew.

"It's all under control, I got you chosen for the Battle of The Bands, didn't I?" says Maddie.

"You did," says Eva, "and how did you do that exactly?"

Yeah Maddie, how *did* you do that?

"I swapped a really cool band's demo with yours, I played it to Tori, she thought the people she was listening to were you, she liked it, you got yourself a place, sweetie!"

"I love it!" says Eva.

Ohmystars, if I hadn't realised these two were related before, I would have done now, except I'd have had them cast as evil twins, not cousins.

"Now all you need to do is fix it so that we win! Those Rainbow freaks will be green with envy!" Oh, that'll be us, then.

"No worries, cuz, here's the plan – go out on stage, click you fingers three times as if you're counting in, I'll flick on the CD and voila, instant rock group!"

They make the noise of showbiz air kisses and say 'yay!' in agreement before leaving the bathroom. I check that the coast is clear before taking a big sigh and opening the cubicle door. I look in the mirror. What was I going to do? If I told anyone the girls would just deny it, if I snuck in and nicked their CD that would make me just as bad as them, and believe it or not, I didn't want to show Eva up, that would just be like me stooping to her level.

But I couldn't just rely on karma-rama taking it's course either, Bella had worked so hard to get us good enough to perform, we'd got here for all the right reasons, not because our cousin worked at *Missy* magazine, yet Eva was going to cheat and walk away with the prize. It just didn't seem right somehow.

I nearly jumped out of my skin when another cubicle clicks open, jeez, Eva really didn't check out her plotting locales, did she? It's Caitlin.

"Oh, thank goodness it's you," she says letting out her own sigh of relief, "were you in here when..."

"Yep, I was," I beat her to it. "I heard everything and, well, they are related, so there's bound to be a chance that they're cut from the same bad girl cloth, right?"

"Maddie is seriously horrible," Caitlin confesses. "She's Tori's assistant and she's nice as pie to Tori's face, but to the rest of us, she's evil kenival." Caitlin explains.

I nod my head. "That sounds about right, Eva is exactly the same, but what can we do about it?" I ask Caitlin. "My gal-pals and I have worked so hard for today and then Eva comes along and is going to ruin everything."

Caitlin smiles, and being a much better plot-planner than Eva and Maddie, she checks the cubicles before pulling herself up onto the counter and telling me her plan in hushed tones. "Well, there's a chance that Maddie *might* get called away to interview The Tooties', you know, just when she should be 'helping' her 'cuz'?"

"Yeah," I nod, "although I think it's slightly wrong that she gets to meet The Tooties' though."

"Ahh, but we need a big enough pull," Caitlin explains, "and I have no doubt she'd choose a celebrity over her own cousin, any day."

"If she's anything like Eva," I say, "then abso-blimmin'-lutely!"

"Anyway," Caitlin continues, "she won't be able to get access because she won't be on the list, but by the time she gets back, it'll be too late to play the CD – what do you think? Are you in?"

"What do I have to do?" I ask.

"Go out there and kick ass, that's all you and your friend's have to do, prove to those girls out there what can happen when you're passionate and determined – leave the rest to me!" I hold my hand up for a Caitlin high-five hoping she wasn't too cool to leave me hanging, she slapped my hand and gave me a wink. She was a total Pink Lady.

Having spent far too much time in the toilet already, I was just about to leave, when rushing past me in a blur of glitter and sparkle was Angel. She ran into the cubicle I'd just come out of, and locked the door.

Sound the dramarama alarm, Angel is in the building.

"I'm not doing it Lo-Lo!" A muffled cry from behind the door announces.

"You're not doing what?" I ask, thinking Bella had asked her to incorporate some crazy new move at the last minute.

"The show Lo, I'm not doing the show..." I hear her crying real tears and feel bad for thinking this is another one of her tantrums. "It's all so big, what if I mess up? What will people say? Nope, I'm not doing it."

"But you've got to do it Angel, you're our unique selling point, even the editor of *Missy* said it!" I say poofing up her ego.

"She did?" Bella ask, sniffing back her tears.

"She did! C'mon, what's really going on Angel-cakes? This isn't like you. Where's my super-confident BFF gone?" I ask sliding up next to the cubicle door. "You've been telling us all day how great you are, and how you couldn't wait to get on stage – what's changed?"

"Lo," she sniffs, "I feel such a fraudster. I know I'm always super confident girl but, I don't know, the last few months with dad going and being at boarding school and well, even hanging around with Bella and Sadie who are so incredibly cool, it's really knocked my confidence."

Colour me stunned.

"That's why I didn't want to be in the band," she went on,

choking a little bit over each word. "Not because I was too cool like I pretended to be, but because I'm not cool enough! I didn't want to be the bad one. The not good enough one."

As Angel was talking, Bella and Sadie had come through the door and I had put my finger to my lips so that Angel would continue talking.

"Hey missy," I say through the door, "I love you 'k? You are totally good enough, you're the tres You-nique Angel Trueman and in moments of self-doubt, you've gotta remember that!"

"We love you too," Sadie says through the door.

"Course we do!" adds Bella, "Look Angel," she continues talking to the door, "I'm sorry if I've been hard on you, I'm such a perfectionist, but that doesn't make it okay, you're fab and I'm so glad to know you and to be in a band with you, c'mon, come out, we're all in this together!"

I didn't think this was the time or the place to point out to Bella that she was now quoting songs from *High School Musical*. Angel unlocked the door and peeped out sheepishly, with big black streams of mascara running down her cheeks. We all grab her in a group hug.

"Come on glam-girl, we can't have you going on stage like that!" I say to her, showing her reflection in the mirror, "let's go back to the room, get yoga dad to teach us a few chill out moves and fix up your mascara!"

"Sorry, guys, I'm such a drama queen, I know," we shake our heads, she nods. "But I know one thing that's worth a bit of drama-rama, we're the Rainbow Hearts, and we rock and rule!"

Now that is a fact.

Chapter twenty one

Make up re-application ☑
Five repetitions of 'We're the Rainbow Hearts and we rock and rule! ☑
Fifteen minutes of yoga stretches ☑

(FYI my favourite is the Lion position – it's fab for letting go of emotions and while you feel beyond silly actually doing it, it loosens your face muscles, melting away tension. Well, if nothing else, it's guaranteed to give you a giggle and yoga-dad says that giggling is the healthiest thing anyone can do, which makes The Pink Ladies and I the healthiest girls ever!)

We were now totes ready to hit the stage, even Angel. Bella has told her if she feels too nervy, just to dance the nerves out, so Angel is now The Rainbow Hearts' tam-tam playing, dancing glam girl, if nothing else we'll most deffo get ten points for originality.

Caitlin gives us a ten minute call but say that if we want to go watch the other band we can and she give me a li'l wink.

"It would be interesting to see what they've got!" I suggest.

We take a final look in the mirror, blow ourselves kisses, and follow Caitlin to the stage. A hustle and bustle of commotion is going on as we pass by The Tootie's dressing room. A girl with a tight pony tail is arguing with a really, really big man.

"But I work for *Missy*," she's exclaiming.

Caitlin rushes us past really quickly and puts her clipboard up near her face to conceal her identity but I totes know who it is. We arrive at the side of the stage to see Eva and the Negative Ninas take to the stage. The crowd are clapping and Eva is loving the attention, throwing her hair around a lot while the Nina's step to their instruments, just as Tori Frankel – eek – announces them, the arguing pony-tailed girl comes rushing past us, makes a dash for the CD player beside the guitar amps, puts the CD in and watches through the curtain as Eva does three finger clicks and she flicks the switch – voila, instant rock band.

Dang it, the plan didn't work. Caitlin and I look at each other in despair while the others are open-mouthed and outraged that this is actually happening. We sneak a peak through the curtain at the audience and they seem to really be enjoying it, in fact it was really good, it sounded just like a song you'd have heard on the radio. While Bella, Sadie, Angel and I all watch them through the curtain, three really pretty girls in black tutu dresses and bright yellow tights march past us and right up on to the stage.

"Shut up! Do you know who that was?" Angel hollers over the music.

"No, who?" I ask, not having a clue but was slightly intrigued as to why they were suddenly storming the stage.

"They're Sugarpop and they're like number 2 in the charts right now!"

"No way!" I shout watching as the girls from Sugarpop head towards the CD player and press the stop button. The crowd are going wild thinking it's part of the act and Eva and The Negative Ninas are still playing, but no sound comes out. Eva's actual real life, not so sweet voice was now reverberating around the whole venue and people were putting their hands over their ears.

What was going on?

Well, it turns out that Eva's cousin Maddie wasn't just super mean, she was super not too bright and had swapped Eva's demo for a not-yet-released Sugarpop single, so Sugarpop, who were supporting The Tootie later in the show, were backstage, heard their not-yet-released single and wondered what was going on. They came to find out, only to discover Eva and the Negative Ninas' miming along to it and trying to pass it off as their own.

Yoga-dad, who has been watching from the wings, comes down beside me and whispers, "What goes around comes around, Lola, it always does," in my ear, which translated into Lola speak, means karmarama really does work. If you do something bad, it really will come back and bite you on the bee-hind, in Eva's case, in a really huge monumentally embarrassing way.

Eva and her Ninas are asked to leave the stage but Eva is kicking and screaming and shouting something about how she couldn't sing live because of acid reflux or something, she shoots me an evil stare as she passes me on the stairs and I can't resist just giving her a wave and saying, "toodle pip!" Not very pink of me, I know, but just a teeny bit sweet as sugar... don't mess with the karmarama!

An apology is made over the loud speaker and the crowd are booing. This is not good. This is not good at all.

Tori Frankel – eek - takes to the stage. "Hi everyone! I am so sorry about that, I promise that Sugarpop will be back later on in the show, and they'll be performing that track how it should be performed...live!" The crowd cheer. Phew.

"In the mean time," she continues, "I'd like you to meet the real winners of Battle of The Band, a band who really do know how to rock, they look great, they sound great, they are great, it's The Rainbow Hearts!"

The crowd cheers as we take to the stage, we plug ourselves in and as Bella reaches down to plug me in I realise that one of the strings on my guitar is broken, it was the one Eva had been 'pretending' to use.

"Bell, Bell!" I whisper still trying to keep a fixed smile so as not to alarm anyone, "my string is broken!"

Bella looks up, takes a deep breath. "Look, we've got no time to change your guitar, but we're not going to let that spoil it for us, ok?" I nod. "But you can't play our song without that string..."

She paused and racked her rock girl brains. "We're going to have to ditch our song, Rainbow Hearts."

Now I know she's gone mad. Bella would never, ever ditch on a chance to be a super star guitar girl for one silly snapped string.

"Chillax dudettes! I do know a song you can play!" Bella laughed. She didn't have to say anymore, because there was one tune I knew I could play with one string if I had to, I loved it that much. Bella mouths our new song choice to the girls and we all did a collective thumbs up – jeez, we were so cheesy sometimes.

Bella played the opening line and together we all channelled our inner Cyndi Lauper – yep, it was our theme tune and as the sound of Bella's voice singing "Girl's Just Wanna Have Fun" filled the venue, girls were dancing in their seats and I even caught sight of Lisa, the red-haired girl from outside who was beaming from ear to ear as she sang along. This was the best feeling in the world. I check in on Angel who is pulling some crazy shapes as she taps her glitter-covered tam-tam on her hip and she smiles.

As Bella strikes the last chord, there is a huge applause and the crowd go wild as Tom Tootie joins us on the stage.

I know.

Tootie Cuti and The Rainbow Hearts on one stage - it was a pink-tinted dream come true!

He was really rather lovely, not the same as he looks in pictures, but lovely none the less.

"Well done, girls, that was an awesome cover," Tom says, talking into a microphone. The crowd are going crazy, he takes Bella's arm and pulls it into the air with his. "The Rainbow Hearts, the winners!"

We all look at each other and do our squeal of joy and happiness, we do it as loud as we possibly can, because right now, we were The Rainbow Hearts and we rocked and ruled!

Chapter twenty two

Things that are making me happy right now
- Eva and The Ninas being escorted off the premises
- Her cousin getting seriously told off by Tori Frankel
- Rocking out on stage in front of hundreds of people
- Winning Battle of The Bands fairly and squarely
- Sitting backstage and shooting the breeze with none other than Tom Tootie – whoop, whoop!

I can't believe that Sadie and I are the ones that are totally cool with the fact that we're kicking back on a worn-out old sofa with Tom Tootie and his band, while Angel and Bella are positively giggle-girl girly about it all.

"You guys are blindin'," Tom tells us as he fiddles with his shoe lace. He's looking at me from behind that floppy fringe and giving me a patented Tom Tootie grin. I think I might pass out.

"Really, you think?" ask Bella practically drowning in her own pool of drool. This, coming from the girl who absolutely, positively did not want to enter the competition and who was going to teach The Tootie's how to play guitar properly.

"Yeah, I do and I love that you bring something different to the mix, I mean I've never seen a band with a dancing tambourine player before – that's so cool!"

"Why thank you, Tom – I think you're rather fabulous too!" gushes Angel, who, this morning didn't even know who The Tootie were and was going to offer up some style tips.

He looks away in a coy way, I'm sure he must have practiced in the mirror, because he really was rather good at it. He trotted it out again when Sadie asked him to sign his poster and there was a definite swoon in the room. This was obviously something he was completely used to, familiar territory, and asked her name he gave her the cutest of grins, she grinned back, it was a totally grin-tastic.

"Tom," I ask, "I know this is really cheeky, but would you mind doing an interview for my zine please?"

"A zine?" he asks. I thought he didn't know what one was so I was about to go into a speech about how it was a cut and paste DIY magazine that I make and fill the pages with all the things I want to, making me the ed-girl of my very own pink domain, but he knows what a zine is, because he used to collect ones about 70's punk bands when he was younger. I tell him that mine are a little more pink than punk and he smiles and says "So what do you want to ask?"

I reach into my bag for my home-made notebook and ask him my here-are-some-I prepared-earlier questions, a journo-girl must be prepared at all times, y'know.

He seems quite shy off stage, I remember reading in an interview once, where he said that the only time he felt really himself was when he was behind a guitar, and that the rest of the time he just felt all awkward and wrong. Which, at the time I didn't really get, what with him being a celeb-boy and all. I mean, celeb-boys were all uber-confident, weren't they? They had to be to go out on stage and rock out, right? But Angel proved today that's not always true and now, sitting in front of Tootie Cuti himself, I can see that he is shy, not at all like the person I see being all bolshy in the music videos.

In fact, I'm not being rude, but Tom Tootie is well... normal. He's deffo really nice to look at, as in really, really nice, but in the same way as magazines use fancy-schmancy computer air-brushing to make celeb-girls look thinner and to have better skin, it turns out they must do the same to boys too, because he didn't look like he did on the poster that Sadie asked him to sign, he just looks, well... normal.

And he seems really normal too. When he's not on stage he wears glasses that make him look prep-boy cute and he reads magazines and newspapers, y'know, just like actual regular people do. I think I'll say it again just so I believe it. Tom Tootie is normal. Still totes cutie patooti, but yep, you've guessed it, normal.

"Boys, you're on!" comes the call of a man with a laminated AAA pass round his neck.

"Cool!" Tom says, jumping to his feet and giving himself a brush down. Seriously, that was the extent of him getting ready. He reaches across to shake our hands and plants a soft sweet Tom Tootie kiss on each of our cheeks. FYI: He didn't smell of flowers and freshly mown grass, but he did smell of deodorant and freshly washed clothes and not dirty, like I imagine most guitar boys smell like. When he kisses Angel's cheek, her legs do a wobble, but she quickly composes herself, before mouthing over his shoulder, "he's so-oo cute!"

With that, he joins his band mates, gives us a final wave before making his way to the stage.

"Er girls," Sadie asks in a super-serious tone. "Do you think it's wrong to take his coke can?" We all laugh out loud but Sadie carefully places the empty can in her tote bag. Whatever makes a chica happy, right?

We shuffle into a row of four seats marked 'reserved for The Rainbow Hearts' just as the lights dim and The Tooties' play the opening chord to 'Girls We Heart'.

Before he sings the first line, Tom Tootie says "I'd like to dedicate this song to a really cool band, you heard them earlier this evening, they're The Rainbow Hearts!"

He whirls his arm like every guitar-playing rock-boy before him and completely takes control of the stage, because that's the magic of music. Tom Tootie, was now most deffo Tootie Cuti and he was singing to us, The Rainbow Hearts!

Think Pink

Issue 2

From the Ed-girl...that's me, Lola Love, btw!

Who'd have funked it, eh?

issue twoOOwoooohhhoo!

Ohmystars! Where's a girl to start? The Pink Ladies and I became a real, kick-ass band The Rainbow Hearts (don't you just love it?), won a comp in *Missy* mag to rock out on stage in front of hundred of people, AND as if that wasn't enough for one pink-tinted girl group, we met THE Tom Tootie!

Yuh-huh.

Not only did we meet him, share the same air space as him, *and* swipe his half-finished can of diet coke — his lips had touched it 'k? - I was actually able to stop myself swoonin' long enough to snag a mucho exclusive interview with the bee-you-tiful faced, guitar-playing, hotster from Hotsville himself.

Sigh.

So, go grab your air guitar, throw your fave rock-girl shape and shake out your best 80's rocker hair-do, because in this issue of *Think Pink*, we are absolutely, positively rockin' out!

Love and pink plectrums...

Lola x

I love mail, email me at: **Lola@lolasland.com**

Five muso-girls/groups i heartoo

Muso girls are radular. Fact.

Check out Bella. When she plays guitar, it's like nothing else in the world matters. For girls-in-music inspir-o, The Rainbow Hearts bow at the kitten heeled feet of *these* girls...

The Pipettes – Gwenno, Rosay and Riot Becki are a retro lovin', polka-dot wearing, all girl vocal harmony trio! They are all about the simultaneous hand moves, mucho catchy harmonies, shaky-shaky pom-poms and adorable flicky hair. Not only do they make achingly cute tuneage, they make us want to apply lashings of pink lipstick and pout. A lot.

Debbie Harry – she's a total iconoclastic muso-girl, if you don't own an album by Debbie or her band, *Blondie*, there's a chance Bella might not actually ever speak to you. Not only did Debbie know how to rock out on stage, she also appeared in the original, uber-cool version of *Hairspray* and made two-tone, bottle blonde hair a totally do-able option. Love you, Debbie.

Shampoo – forget The Spice Girls, these blonde-haired, teen queens were the original tiara-wearin', Hello Kitty lovin', princesses of all things Girl Power. Go Youtube them right away – Viva La Megababes!

Sahara Hot Nights – They might be from Sweden but this 4 piece all-girl rock band ain't no Abba! They're a combo of garage rock, power punk and poppy-pop - they're our total idol girls – I'm currently working at growing a chunky-monkey, in-your-eyes fringe ala guitarist/singer Maria Andersson!

Chrissie Hynde – she's an Americano singing, guitar-playing, songwriting, lady-legend of girls-in-music! If you looked up 'totally amazing rock goddess' in the dictionary, there will be a picture of Chrissie Hynde right next to it. Fact.

Honouree mention: Jem and The Holograms –

not technically a real band, in fact it's a retro 1980s cartoon about a singer named Jem, her band, The Holograms, and their adventures. It's allsorts of awesome - Jem has neon pink hair and uses catch phrases like "Showtime, Synergy!" and "Truly outrageous!" – what's not to love about that??

Make your own journo-girl notebook

Forget rushing to buy a new notebook to jot down all your journo-girl needs, it's far, far cooler to make your own!

You'll need:

A boring snorin' notebook

A cool 'all about you' cover

Scissors

Glue

The cover is the cool bit – it can be absolutely anything you want it to be – I suggest hitting up the chazza shops to grab a few old record albums. FYI: Records are those big black circular things that used to play music before CDs – retro-tastic. Look for titles that make you smile or speak to you. Like the 'Grease' soundtrack or "Disco Fever".

Rip the album cover apart so you have a front and back.

Now, cut two pieces, one from the front of the album jacket, the other from the back, the size of your notebook and stick them to your borin' snorin' notebook – voila insta-one-of-a-kind notebook to impress ll your interviewees with!

Tootie Cuti!

Tom Tootie is most deffo a 100% certified cutie! How do I know? Because I got the chance to hang out with him and his band, The Tooties backstage! Sigh. Thud.

First off, tell us all how The Tooties' got together...

My brother James and I started playing guitar when we were young – we loved The Ramones and wanted to be like them so badly! We'd do little shows for our family and mates, maybe playing one or two songs. When people said they actually liked our stuff, we decided to form a band with our school buds, Chan and Joey and started sharing the music with a bigger audience.

You're famous for being lovely to your fans – what makes your fans so special?

We have the most amazing following! It's more like a family, really. We love being able to make a personal connection with our fans.

Well, The Rainbow Hearts are very glad that you did, Tom!

It's something I always wanted to do as a kid – to meet my favourite bands – and I never really got to do it, but I think it's nice to give something back. Our fans have been so great to us. They're the best fans in the world.

What's the best bit about being in a band?

Being on stage, it's such a buzz!

What makes The Tooties' different from every other guitar band out there?

We're larger than life – not literally, obviously - because actually, we're really quite small, but we're definitely not a boring jeans and t-shirt band! On stage we love to dress up, wear glitter and do something a little different, y'know?

Don't you just love him?! Sigh. Thud. *Again*.

The Rainbow Hearts

Meet The Rainbow Hearts
– Lola, Sadie, Bella and
Angel - we rock and rule –
and this is our sweeter
than sweet 5-point
manifesto for our being the
best girl band, EVAH!

Smile – In
pictures and in
person, a smile
makes you so
much more
likeable.
Athough Bella is
allowed to pull
her trade-mark
punk-girl snarl
during any
guitar solo.

Being a loud mouth isn't a necessity – Don't bad mouth other bands, even if they're not very good, just to get attention. *Show* people what you're about rather than shouting it in their faces.

Don't be too serious – We want to meet Tom Tootie, and we want to be a kick-butt girl band, but more importantly, we're going to have lots of fun doing it - yeah!

Own the stage – Tell yourself how fabulous you are at five times in the mirror, give yourself a hug o' love and walk out on stage and own it.

Remember that girls who rock, rock hardest! - We're girls and we rock – that's the most rocking-est thing, ever!

The Rainbow Hearts fast faves:
Colour: Pink, natch.
Song: Cyndi Lauper – Girl's Just Want To Have Fun
Food: Chocolate – yumsville city!
Crush: Tom Tootie – he's so hot he could melt a million hearts.

How to chill:
The Lion position

For messy, stressy times when you need to keep your cool – try this fab yoga position...

Kneel on the floor with your knees a shoulder-width apart, or slightly wider.

Sit back on your heels and place your hands on your knees.

Keeping your back straight, inhale and lean forwards, resting your hands on the floor between your knees if it's easier.

Now comes the fun part – stretch your mouth and jaw as wide as possible, sticking out your tongue as far as you can. Focus your gaze on the tip of your tongue as you tense and straighten your fingers, like lion claws.

Hold this pose for one breath, then relax. Repeat five times with a short break in between each one

Ask Lola

Not only am I writer-girl and now celeb meeting, guitar-girl too, I also like to think of myself as a pink-thinkin', sparkle princess of wiseness – go on, ask me anything!

I want to play the drums, but my dad says 'it's just a phase' and won't let me, what shall I do?

It's no wonder you want to play the drums - beat makin' girls are coolio-a-go-go! Pink Lady Sadie's idol girl is Meg

White from The White Stripes, Meg's parents didn't dig her playing the drums right away either, but like her, you have to prove to your parentals how serious you are about it. Find out how much a class is and save up for it with your own pocket money, let your Dad know you're doing it and he'll soon see that you mean business!

My bff and I have been best buds since we were tiny. Recently, I've taken up dancing and have made some new friends, my best friend has got really weird about it and doesn't want me to hang out with them – I like them both and don't want to have to choose...

It sounds like your bff is feeling a little insecure and is probably worried you might not wanna hang with her now you have new friends. Start by letting her know, that no matter what, you think she rocks and even though you're making new friends, doesn't mean you're gonna dump your old ones. Offer to introduce her to your dancing buds over a game of bowling or a bite to eat – keep it fun!

I've been cast as the lead in the school play, which is a dream come true, but I get stage fright, how can I find the confidence to stand on stage?

Congrats on bagging the leading role!

A little bit of nervous energy is good as

it gives you the boost you need to give a

stellar performance on the night, but

the trick is, not to let it take over. Tell

yourself in the mirror how great you

are five times over before going on

stage, hold your head high, take deep

breaths and go get 'em, chica!

How to: play the guitar

Bella is a guitar playin' goddess, she taught me to play C, A and D chords in one evening by writing numbers on my left hand...

You wanna learn too?

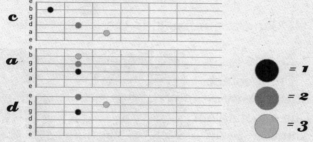

Number your fingers on your left hand with a felt tip then, starting with chord C, it's the easiest, match it up with the beautifully drawn chart. The lines going down are strings, the lines going across are frets, put your fingers in position and with your right hand, strum!

Practice, practice, practice each one, then when you feel comfy, start playing them faster and together until you can switch between different chords without having to think about it...You're officially a guitar girl – woohoo!

A Lola paper doll – Rock girl

I'm a combo of the Truly Outrageous Jem and the ultimate guitar goddess of ALL time, Joan Jett – rock out!

Hey chicas, join me and the Pink Ladies in our ultimate guides to Thinking Pink!

If you're looking for somewhere fun, fabulous and totally you-nique on the web? Come and hang with me, Bella, Angel and Sadie at Lolasland.com!

We've got news, reviews, interviews as well as beauty, fashion, games and more. You can even build your very own Lola's Land – c'est tres chic!

Looking forward to seeing you there, **chica!**